LAZONBY'S HEIRESS

Melanie Brightman

Safe Sex is essential: your very life may depend on it. Please remember that some of the sexual practices that are featured in this work of fiction (written in an era that pre-dates lethal STDs) are dangerous and they are not recommended or in any way endorsed by the publishers; by the same token, we do not condone any form of non-consensual sex for any reason: it is reprehensible and illegal and should never become a part of a person's real life: rather it should remain firmly in the realm of sexual fantasy.

THE *Erotic* Print Society
London 2003
Reprinted December 2003

THE *Erotic* Print Society
EPS, 1 Maddox Street
LONDON W1S 2PZ

Tel (UK only): 0800 026 25 24
Fax: +44 (0)20 7437 3528
Email: eros@eroticprints.org
Web: www.eroticprints.org

© 2003 MacHo Ltd, London UK

ISBN : 1-898998-70-1

LAZONBY'S HEIRESS

Melanie Brightman

THE *Erotic* Print Society

Foreword by Michael R. Goss

The history of erotic literature has always been clandestine, and, apart from furtive purchases of under-the-counter hardcore, American readers between the end of the war and the mid-1960s could only openly buy paperbacks with lurid covers that always promised, like first dates, far more than they actually delivered. However, the sale of two trashy paperbacks at a news-stand in New York's Times Square was to change the history of erotic publishing in the United States forever.

Previously there had been several landmark cases involving the publication of books that extended the boundaries of what was legally acceptable. These included James Joyce's *Ulysses*, D.H. Lawrence's *Lady Chatterley's Lover*, Henry Miller's *Tropic of Cancer*, John Cleland's *Memoirs of a Woman of Pleasure* and William Burrough's *Naked Lunch*. All novels which today we celebrate and study as major works of literature.

The pivotal moment came when Robert Redrup, a Times Square newsstand clerk, sold two pulp sex novels, *Lust Pool* and *Shame Agent* to plain-clothes policeman, for which he was tried and convicted in 1965.

William Hamling, who published the books under his Nightstand imprint in San Diego, paid Redrup's legal bills to the Supreme Court and the resulting case, *Redrup v. New York* in May 1967, truly opened the floodgates of what was acceptable.

Hamling, and his lawyer Stanley Fleishman, firmly believed that he was not selling, as was said about his books, "commercialised obscenity," nor would he admit to "titillating the prurient interests of people with a weakness for such expression." Hamling felt his books were giving people who would never have the skills to read and enjoy *Ulysses*, *Fanny Hill* or *Naked Lunch* what they wanted.

The judge presiding over the case of Redrup, Justice Potter Stewart, went far beyond his established just-left-of-centre position on obscenity to the most radical of outlooks. Apparently the vote to affirm Ralph Ginzburg's conviction for his magazine *Eros* was his personal wake-up call. In his Ginzburg summary Stewart wrote:

Censorship reflects a society's lack of confidence in itself. It is a hallmark of an authoritarian regime. Long ago those who wrote our First Amendment charted a different course. They believed a society can be truly strong only when it is truly free. In the realm of expression they put their faith, for better or worse, in the enlightened choice of the people, free from the interference of a policeman's intrusive thumb or a judge's heavy hand. So it is that the Constitution protects coarse expression as well as refined, and vulgarity no less than elegance. A book worthless to me may convey something of value to my neighbour. In the free society to which our Constitution has committed us, it is for each to choose for himself.

Stewart's arguments were persuasive enough to convince the court to reverse Redrup's original conviction by 7-2. This decision by the United States Supreme Court affirmed that consenting adults ought to be constitutionally entitled, under the First Amendment, to acquire and read any publication that they wished, including those agreed to be obscene or pornographic, free of interference from the U.S. Government.

Under this guiding principle the Supreme Court adopted a policy of systematically reversing without further opinion ("Redruping") all obscenity convictions which reached it. Scores of obscenity rulings involving paperback sex books, girlie magazines and peep shows were overturned.

Despite an attempt to reverse the tide of pornography by new Chief Justice Warren E. Burger in the 1970s an explosion in paperback publishing followed. Carpet-bagger publishers burst into life across America, including Brandon House, Essex House, Lancer, Midwood, Pendulum, Pleasure Readers and many others. Every aspect of human sexuality was covered in a sexual anarchy of threesomes, foursomes and more-somes in every combination of genders and colours, often including the whole family, their pets and assorted farm animals to boot. Every genre was exploited from incest to Nazi sex with everything in-between in a total assault on the values of bourgeois culture. One can imagine publishers and authors sitting in bars coming up with titles in alcohol-and dope-fuelled brainstorming sessions which would then be commissioned out to a stable of jobbing hacks for around $200 a book.

Past Venus Press will reissue the highlights from this post-Redrup period, many of which were originally considered to have had no literary merit whatsoever and to be utterly without redeeming social importance. But that, of course, was part of their charm.

Chapter 1

One May evening, alone in her bedsit in Chelsea, Alison Jeffreys had come across the small advertisement when she was scanning the classified ads in a London paper. Though she already had a job – had held it for six months, in fact – with a firm of London solicitors, she still continued to glance, albeit casually, at openings for secretarial assistants.

'Secretary,' the ad had said, 'for country estate management, rental, etc. Top salary, accommodation and board in fine old Somerset residence. Age 21-25, single and unattached. Please enclose recent photo with application to Mrs. Hermione Simpson, Lazonby Hall, Nether Maidensgrove, Somerset.'

Alison had read it twice, then thought about it. She was the right age, twenty-three, and she was single – and, she added to herself with a trace of bitterness, completely unattached.

Indeed, since Jonathan had walked out on her two weeks ago, she couldn't have been more unattached! So maybe, just maybe, a change of scenery would be good for her morale.

The pretty brunette sighed. If this were a potential employer who was male, she thought, there would be more of a chance. She was perfectly well aware of her good figure and attractive face. Although on the petite side at just over five feet tall, Alison knew that she was a pocket Venus – with curves in all the right places, large, expressive hazel eyes and the sort of bust that all women envied. But there would probably be lots of applicants, and there was little chance that she'd be selected. Nevertheless, Alison wrote a careful application, enclosed a snap (Jonathan had taken it during the summer) and posted everything off.

Two weeks later, when she had almost forgotten about her application, she got a reply.

And what made this reply different was the fact that a postal order – enough to cover her train fare plus an extra ten pounds for expenses – was enclosed with the letter.

"I'd like to meet you," Mrs. Simpson had written, "and if you like Lazonby, and everything else is satisfactory, then..."

Alison had read the letter very carefully, then decided that a trip to Somerset, all expenses paid, would not be such a bad idea, so she'd phoned – as Mrs. Simpson had also suggested – then made the journey on the Saturday following.

A small, stocky man, wearing a chauffeur's cap, met her at Nether Maidensgrove station. He introduced himself as Sean O'Toole, her employer's chauffeur, butler and handyman; Alison smiled at the intense 'Irishness' of his name but in fact his voice bore only a faint, lilting brogue – which she found rather attractive. He drove her through Nether Maidensgrove in a large silver-grey Bentley.

It had just finished raining and the Somerset countryside had looked wonderful after the noise and dust of London; as they rounded the bend in the drive, she caught a glimpse of the manor itself: one of those delightful, sprawling English houses of uncertain date, so over-clad with ivy and wisteria that it was almost impossible to determine any clues as to its true architectural period.

O'Toole opened the massive, studded, oak front door and together they crossed the marble checker-board floor of the large entrance hall to the base of a broad staircase that led up to the drawing-room landing.

Hermione Simpson was a tall, elegant and slightly forbidding woman of about forty-five. Her rich chestnut hair, flecked with grey, was done up at the back in a tight bun held in place by a pair of green jade pins. After the usual polite formalities, she got straight to the point.

"There really isn't a great deal of work involved," she said. "And since my husband died several years ago, I've managed everything myself – but now I feel I'd like to have someone take charge of everything for me." She laughed. "Maybe I'm getting lazy in my old age."

You don't look so old, Alison had thought, although your manner is certainly that of a rather older person.

What she'd learned of the job, Alison had liked. There were a dozen or so houses on the estate, which had been rented to the same people for years – and half a dozen more that were rented out seasonally.

When Mrs. Simpson mentioned the salary, Alison's eyes had opened wide. It was higher than she was getting in town – and all her living expenses would be taken care of here, too!

"Do you have any family?" she had asked, hesitantly, thinking that there might be more work involved.

"Only my daughter, Jillian," said Hermione Simpson.

"Oh!" Alison had wondered. A daughter!

Would I be expected to baby-sit, too? Is that the fly in the ointment?

"How... how old is Jillian, Mrs. Simpson? Is she here?" she had asked, wondering if she was being too bold.

"Nineteen," Mrs. Simpson had startled Alison by answering. "I think she's somewhere outside. She's a rather... original girl and keeps to herself a lot of the time."

Alison had nodded thoughtfully. If she has a 'difficult' daughter, that could explain why she wants someone to help with the estate. It might also explain why I haven't seen any other members of the family.

* * *

She had told Mrs. Simpson that she would think about it; thanked her for the pre-paid trip and promised to call her, but by the time the train had rolled from lush countryside to the unprepossessing outskirts of the city, Alison had already made up her mind.

She had phoned Mrs. Simpson on Sunday, who sounded pleased at her decision, given her notice at work on Monday, and by the following week was ready to make her move.

Sean O'Toole met Alison again, touching his cap respectfully when she alighted from the train, and then carrying her meagre luggage to the waiting Bentley.

It was an old car, Alison realised as they drove along the twisting Somerset lanes and through the high, dense hedgerows toward Lazonby Hall. Old, but beautifully kept – then she glanced at the back of the driver's head. It would be hard to say how old Sean O'Toole was, Alison decided; he could be anything from thirty-five to forty-five. Certainly a little older than the car, she thought to herself, smiling. His face was tanned and weather-beaten, and his short, sturdy body looked tough and durable.

Alison frowned critically. Although not quite her ideal of the tall, unctuous chauffeur – he seemed more the stocky, outdoors type – his presence was somehow both very male and reassuring.

"Do you work for Mrs. Simpson full-time?" she asked.

He jerked his head up as though he was surprised at being addressed.

"Yes, Miss." He slowed at a crossing, then went on, "I drive and work in the grounds as well as serve at table."

She nodded. It was just as she thought.

"Miss – it's Miss Jeffreys, isn't it?" the driver asked.

"Yes," she told him, "Alison Jeffreys." She smiled.

"Did you..." he asked very slowly, "...meet young Miss Jillian when you were here before?"

"Why, no," she said. "She's a bit of a loner, isn't she?"

Sean O'Toole made a sound that could have been a laugh, then said, "She keeps herself to herself all right, but," his eyes flickered to hers in the driving mirror, "she's not exactly a shrinking violet."

"What makes you say that?" Alison was startled.

Sean shrugged. "It's hard to say really, Miss. She's just not quite like other young women of her age... boisterous, even tomboyish, you might say, I suppose – and sometimes she doesn't really act as a girl of her age should." There was a slight edge of irony to his normally lilting voice.

Alison's eyebrows rose. She wondered what she was missing here. "You mean she's a bit... backwards?"

Sean didn't answer for a while, then said, "Backwards? Lord, no, Miss! Better you find out for yourself, Miss." He swallowed. "It's just that Mrs. Simpson wouldn't want me to talk about... that is... it's not really my place to talk about Miss Jillian!" he finally blurted out. And they finished the drive to the manor in silence.

This time a cheerful, bustling woman in her late twenties or early thirties opened the imposing front door of Lazonby Hall. She was buxom and blonde, and Alison couldn't help but find her broad, sunny smile, rosy cheeks and creamy complexion enormously attractive.

"Welcome to Lazonby Hall," she said to Alison, her voice sweet and thick as cream, with its soft West Country burr. "I'm Rosie Williams, the cook and housekeeper – Mrs. Simpson is resting just now and she asked me to show you to your room."

Alison smiled in reply, murmured a few words, and then followed the cook through the tall, spacious hall. Sean O'Toole followed with Alison's luggage.

Now, as they mounted the wide stairway that curved in a majestic sweep towards the next floor, Alison had time to glance at the numerous portraits that hung there. Unless these were 'instant ancestors', purchased by the square yard, the Simpson family seemed to be a very old one, stretching back for many generations, she decided. Her room overlooked a large, rambling garden at the back, flooded by the golden afternoon sun and full of mature, spreading trees that cast long shadows on the neatly tended lawns, colourful flowerbeds and dense herbaceous borders.

"What a lovely room!" cried Alison, surveying the light, airy bedroom. With its generously swagged chintz curtains, deep-pile carpet and tasteful wallpaper against which were hung fine botanical prints, it was hardly the garret she had been expecting: more the room of a favoured guest. There was an antique dressing-table and mirror with a covering of fine white lace; the bed looked invitingly soft and new.

"Your bathroom is en suite," said Rosie, opening a door at the side that revealed a fully equipped modern bathroom.

Alison nodded with pleasure, then asked, "And is this a closet?" She indicated another door at the side of the bathroom door.

The cook shook her head. "That's just a spare room – the door is always locked," she said briefly.

Alison glanced at the door casually, noticing that the glass transom above it was curtained from the other side; then she turned away, dismissing it from her mind.

* * *

On the other side of the door, someone stood

on the seat of a chair, and kept silent; the whole of Alison's room was visible through a little gap in the curtains. Quivering with impatience, the hidden observer waited for Rosie and O'Toole to leave the bedroom.

When the door had closed behind the two servants, Alison dropped onto the satin-covered bed and, with a contented smile on her lovely face, let her body sink into the softness.

Her watcher's body became tense. Alison's brief skirt had worked up while she was squirming on the bed, and from behind the transom, the thin silk of her panties stretching across the plump 'v' of the newcomer's pudendum could be seen. A shadow of darkness, like brunette pubic hair, seemed just visible through the sheer silk. The watcher's hand slid downwards.

Suddenly, Alison slipped her legs off the bed, then scrambled across to her luggage and hefted a suitcase onto the bedside chair.

She opened it, took out a conservative, dark blue dress and looked at it quizzically. After a moment, she threw the dress onto the bed, snapped shut her suitcase and started to unbutton her blouse.

The watcher's tongue slid out between dry lips, wetting them with jerky, excited little licks.

Alison's flesh appeared so soft and smooth as she shrugged out of her blouse; she unhooked her brassiere, threw it onto the bed and cupped her generous, naked breasts. The watcher gasped: they were quite the most beautiful breasts ever! Large (but not too large) and wonderfully tip-tilted, their prominent nipples were set against broad, light pinky-brown areolae. From behind the door, the watcher's own hand moved silently to tweak a pair of small, but already prominent nipples into a state of delicious sensitivity, as if imagining what it would be like to pinch and squeeze the young woman's tender buds.

Now the firm tips of Alison's nipples could be seen peeping between her fingers. Her admirer swallowed with an effort.

Alison had moved in front of the full-length mirror; she stared at her reflection as she gently caressed her firm, creamy mounds. Her eyes briefly closed and her lips pursed into an expression of pleasure as she felt the warm, yielding flesh undulate under her fingertips.

Reluctantly, Alison slid her hands off her full breasts, reached to the waist of her skirt, unzipped it and slid it off.

The watcher took a deep breath and devoured the sight of the new secretary's full, beautifully rounded buttocks, tightly encased in the silk of her panties, then gazed avidly at them as Alison slipped her fingers in the waistband, gently tugging the flimsy garment down off her hips and legs.

As Alison leaned forward, the cleft in her bottom opened then closed, revealing, for a split-second, the walnut-brown rosette of her anus; this was enough to cause the watcher's hand to grope blindly downwards in an attempt to satisfy a burgeoning lust.

Alison turned around, showing the thick, silken thatch of brown pubic hair at the base of her creamy, softly curving belly; showing, too, wet, pink lips that rubbed gently against each other as she moved.

The watcher's eyes were glued to the pale, shimmering thighs and the exciting pink slit between. This entrancing sight caused the watcher's hand to move more rapidly now, caressing genitals that were engorged, aroused and begging for attention.

Alison picked up the blue dress, held it in front of her naked body, and scrutinised herself in the mirror. Her back was turned, and the watcher could see the gentle muscular movement of her thighs and her buttocks as Alison swayed back and forth, slightly raised, on the balls of her feet.

The watcher's excitement increased, the hand moving more quickly still.

Alison walked back to the bed, blue dress in her hand, and then sat on the edge, staring at the dress thoughtfully. After a moment she dropped onto her back, legs dangling over the side of the bed, and let the dress slip out of her hand.

Her thighs parted, then she stroked the insides of her legs with slow, lingering sweeps. Slowly, her hands moved higher – her thighs parted even wider – and the wonderful pink gash of Alison's sexual parts could be seen to stretch wide open.

The lusty young woman, blissfully unaware of her exposure, delicately traced the wavy line of a wet inner lip with the tip of her finger; a tremor ran through her flesh. Her eyes closed, then she jerked up her heels until they were propped on the edge of the bed. Her knees fell apart and she stabbed a stiffened finger into the soft, spongy wetness of her vaginal tunnel.

The figure behind the door was treated to the sight of Alison's finger sinking into her soaking wet flesh: it seemed as if her vagina were sucking it in, drawing her digit inward, deeper and deeper like a hungry mouth.

Then Alison's fingers slipped either side of her luscious slit and gently pulled back: a small, pink bud popped out from the top of her clitoral hood and she used her other hand to touch, press and squeeze it with exquisite pleasure. Her mouth opened and closed as she drew in gulps of air.

From the other side of the transom the watcher, slack-jawed and also breathing raggedly, was becoming aware of an impending climax: both the watcher's hands were feverishly working tormented genital flesh towards orgasm.

Alison had lifted her buttocks, and thrust her finger in deeper, only to pull it out wetly, dragging the pink, clinging flesh with it. Her clitoris had grown larger and she tormented the rubbery, pink, bean-sized organ with her finger and thumb, pinching it, pulling it and squeezing. Her hips began to buck gently up and down.

Behind the door the chair began to shake.

Alison was masturbating with frenetic movements; her thighs spread smoothly open and between them her little bud seemed to squirm and writhe as she teased it and pleased it, tormented and titillated it, with soft, then vicious, manipulations.

The watcher's excitement, too, was building to a massive climax, hands moving in a blur, as if in sympathy with the frantic actions of the girl on the bed.

Alison's eyes opened wide, her pupils dilated and she drew in her cheeks, biting them gently with her teeth as she squeezed on the tip of her clitoris. Then the spasms started: blasting through her flesh, making her legs writhe – thighs slapping closed then jerking open – as she slammed her fingers deep inside her soaking vulva. Suddenly, a high wail came from her lips reaching the watcher's ears faintly through the transom as the young girl reached orgasm and her vagina gushed a flood of clear liquid, creating a dark patch on the bedcover.

Consumed by violent orgasm, the watcher's hips, too, started to buck and twitch; more liquid spattered against the door to Alison's room.

The watcher saw Alison's body relaxing, her eyes closing in satiation as a sudden languor seemed to spread through her body. Vaginal fluid still oozed from between her swollen, livid labia; the watcher observed it all greedily, almost proprietarily.

"Ohh... Alison – so you're a squirter. Now I really *must* have you!"

Chapter 2

"So she's the secretary," said the cook to the chauffeur.

He shrugged, gave a sardonic smile. "That's what Hermione says."

"I didn't see her when she was here before. She's such a pretty young girl," said Rosie.

They were talking in the kitchen. Rosie's hands and arms were covered in white flour; she was preparing a meal, while Sean O'Toole was sipping a glass of beer.

"Naturally," he said, "she wouldn't have got one that wasn't nice looking." He took a gulp of his drink, then added as an afterthought, "Sexy figure, too."

Rosie answered with her back to the chauffeur. "I suppose so." She paused, then: "D'you think… that she's got her for…?"

Sean shrugged. "What else?"

Rosie continued with her work, then she murmured, "I feel sort of sorry for her, although…" she hesitated, "…in some ways I can't say I am sorry."

Sean jerked his head up: the pretty, buxom cook was blushing, her eyes downcast.

"I suppose it'll make things easier for you," he muttered. "Take some of the load off you." There was a bitter note in his voice.

Rosie's flush became deeper. "Something like that," she whispered.

"The monster!" Sean spat out the words.

"Why do you put up with it?"

Rosie didn't answer his question. "D'you know what I got last night?" she asked in a shocked whisper.

"You don't have to tell me," Sean murmured.

Rosie put her lips close to Sean's ear and whispered, "I got it right up the back of me," she hissed. "Right into my bottom," she panted with emotion, "my... my arse cheeks prised open and that big thing stuck in me. I – I thought it was going to tear me wide open... oh, how it burned me as it pushed into me." Rosie's hand went behind her and she stroked the generous curve of her buttocks tenderly, as though she could still feel the huge, stiff intrusion forcing itself into her tight anal pucker.

"Then I had to get on top and was made to go up and down, up and down. It was horrible, really it was."

"Why?" Sean forced out the word. "I mean – why up your backside?"

Rosie hung her head and breathed out the shame-filled words. "It seems that I'm not 'tight' enough: my arsehole's tight enough but my pussy isn't, apparently." She looked down and her voice went even lower. "I think it's just pure, spiteful wickedness, though."

"They're monsters, all of them!" Sean's

face was pale with anger. He reached out for Rosie, encircling her waist with his muscular arm. "Why... why d'you let them?"

Rosie stroked Sean's head absently. "You – you know why – you know what they – what Hermione – pays me!"

He didn't answer.

"How much d'you think I'd get for just being a cook?" she asked, bitterly. "You know that I have to do it." She bent down, looking into Sean's face. "And you do things, too, Sean – Hermione makes you do things, too, doesn't she?"

"That's different," he mumbled. He slipped his hand under Rosie's skirt, found bare thigh-flesh, then slid his fingers inside her panties, and caressed her. "I have to do it to keep my job!"

Rosie heard his words but she was thinking of something else. "I suppose that's why they got her," she murmured.

Sean didn't follow her. "What?"

"This young girl – this secretary – I suppose that's what she's for! A nice snug cunt to fuck – so dear Mrs. Simpson goes out and gets one."

"She's a nasty bitch, our employer," sighed Sean. "We should stop it – we should warn the poor girl." But his words lacked conviction.

Rosie shook her head. "You know we can't do that," she said quietly. "Anyway, I suppose she's being well paid for it."

Sean squeezed Rosie's ample buttocks, then drew his finger up the cleft. Rosie flinched. "Was that Doctor there?" Sean asked.

Rosie smiled ruefully. "Not this time, no."

"He's a nasty piece o' work, too," said Sean again, remembering. "If I had my way, I'd castrate the bastard."

She reached down to Sean's crotch, squeezing at the fleshy bulge through his trousers.

"I'm glad you're not castrated," she said with a half-giggle.

He managed a grin. "You'll be gladder still tonight."

"Don't brag," she murmured, then she asked, "I wonder if this girl'll be willing to do what they want."

"Whether she's willing or not, she'll do it." Sean looked at Rosie.

"They have ways. You know that – you ought to know that!"

"You mean the Doctor will take care of it again?"

"You shouldn't call him 'Doctor', he isn't a Doctor any more – he was struck off. Hermione knows something about him – that's why he does what she tells him."

"I suppose…"

"Miss Alison's young cunt will be screwed tonight, you can be sure of that." Sean spoke slowly, almost deliberately. "Squeezing that great thing into that snug, tight pussy."

The voluptuous blonde cook drew in her breath and her pelvis jerked forward. "Why, Sean! You're getting me all excited talking like that!" she whispered.

Sean pressed his fingers into her full, resilient buttocks, pulling her body against his so that she could feel the hardness of his penis jammed into her flesh.

"D'you have to wait until tonight?" she whispered.

He shook his head, running his lips over her cheek until his mouth came to her pretty pink ear. His tongue flicked out and ran around the delicate contours, darting quickly in so that her whole body shuddered with pleasure.

Rosie pulled herself back, her face alive with excitement. "Not here," she murmured, dragging Sean to the side of the kitchen. "We can do it in the larder." She opened the door to the small storage room with its slightly musty, sweet odour of hams and cheeses. "No one but me ever goes in here." He slid into the tiny place, let Rosie close the door behind them with a click and stared at her in the dimness. She hoicked her skirt up at the front, then clawed at her crotch with bruising, urgent fingers.

Sean watched her panties slide down and when the thick growth of blonde pubic hair became visible, he ripped his trousers open and pulled out his swollen penis.

Rosie's glance veered down onto the still thickening shaft, then she jammed her buttocks on a low shelf so that she was in a half-squatting position. She spread her thighs wide open and through the golden curls of her pubic bush, Sean could see the swollen, rosy folds of her labia.

"Mmm… what a lovely wet, fucking cunt," he muttered, taking a shaky step closer to the woman.

"Don't talk – just do me!" Rosie slid her fingers down, pulling open the lips of her vulva.

Sean moved between the open thighs, feeling Rosie's hands on his belt, unfastening it, letting his trousers slip down; then her fingers were clutching his buttocks and pulling his body closer to her, deep into her, with hungry strength.

He gripped the shaft of his penis, steering the jerking head into the wet mass of sexual flesh. The walls of her vulva gripped the sides of his cock, seeming to suck it up and into her body.

"Ohhh, Rosie," Sean groaned, "your pussy's so hot and ready for it!"

She pressed her mouth on his, and sucked and nibbled at his lips as she felt the hard shaft penetrate her deeply. "Oh yes... your lovely long, hard cock," she growled. "You're filling me... all of me; you're fucking your cock right up into my belly!"

She jerked herself down, and the stiff cock travelled further inside her vagina. "Like that," she moaned, writhing. "Go on – do it! Fuck me, do me hard, yes, like that!"

Sean's knees trembled when he bent them to let his cock slide down, then he drove inside again, deeper and deeper, feeling the walls of Rosie's vagina undulating against his throbbing shaft. "Oooh, you sweet fuck," he murmured, trembling with excitement, "you're suckin' the spunk out of me!"

"Keep fucking, don't stop!" she said, her voice urgent, ragged. She tried to squeeze her thighs together to heighten the sensation and the movement of her thigh muscles tightened the grip of her vagina.

"Oooh, sweet Jesus!" Sean panted, feeling the wet grip on the shaft of his cock. "Keep holding my John Thomas like that!"

He lurched himself upward, his cock making wet, sensuous sounds as it thrust through the soaking flesh; then he dragged the shaft down, feeling Rosie's body quivering against his as the thrills throbbed through her flesh.

"Oh, Sean-lad – don't stop, you lovely man!" Rosie panted out the words breathlessly and squirmed her buttocks on the edge of the shelf as she sucked at his cock with her pulsating pussy.

Sean could feel the head of his cock expanding and contracting and molten rivulets of juice began to spasm inside his balls.

"Rosie," he gasped, "I'm gonna... gonna... blow!" His voice rose and his in-and-out movements became frenzied.

"Sean, sweet Sean!" Rosie tried to stifle the squeal that rose in her throat as his swollen organ jammed against the tip of her stiffening clitoris. She wriggled herself urgently, working the hard clitoral tip on the swelling, throbbing shaft.

Thrills flickered through her vaginal walls then cascaded through every part of her sexual flesh. "I'm coming!" she grunted, then her teeth bit gently on Sean's sensitive earlobe as the orgasm hit her hard, jerking her pelvis and feeling her whole cunt quiver in spontaneous reaction.

"Urgh, Rosie – *Rosieee!*" Sean's voice rose high as burning spurts of thick sperm squirted from the tip of his cock, spattering against the flesh at the top of Rosie's vagina, scalding her, thrilling her and making her flesh shiver until she lifted her feet off the floor, wedged herself on the edge of the shelf and wrapped her legs around Sean with her heels jammed into his buttocks, pulling him ever deeper inside her sexual cavern.

At last, her mouth moved away from Sean's, her teeth relinquished their grip on his ear and she panted, "You lovely big cock, oooh, Sean – you drive me bloody wild you do!"

"Holy Mother of God!" he mumbled, feeling the last dregs of juice trickle from the end of his cock. "Your cunt was just built for fucking!"

She gave a breathless giggle, and leaned against him, feeling his softening shaft sliding out of her. "I came, Sean O'Toole," she whispered. "You always make me come – and…" she hesitated, then buried her face on his shoulder so that her words were muffled, "and now, will you suck me, Sean?"

"Hungry pussy," he muttered, "always ready for more!" But he obeyed, letting his body drop down until his face was level with her belly. She opened her thighs eagerly, then reached down and stretched the lips of her pussy wide open. He watched in awe as his deposit of pearly sperm began to ooze out. The pink, tensed head of her clitoris slid into view and Sean took a deep breath, bent his head and opened his mouth.

"Like that!" Rosie breathed as his lips encircled her clitoral tip. "Suck it into your mouth – tickle it with your tongue – bite it, Sean!"

He gripped the squirming little nub with his teeth, pulling it away from its warm, wet slot.

Rosie made low, ecstatic sounds and entwined her fingers in the hair on Sean's bent head.

"Go on... please stick your tongue up my pussy," she begged in a whisper.

He drove his tongue into her, tasting the saltiness of the creamy mixture of his and her come-juice, then sucked at her clitoris again.

Bubbling moans poured from Rosie's lips and she rocked herself, slowly and sensuously, as Sean licked, sucked and bit with thrilling sexual devotion.

"I'm going to come again!" The words exploded from Rosie's lips; her whole body convulsed and shuddered violently and she almost jerked her clitoris from the light grip of Sean's teeth.

"Now!" she gasped, her eyes wide open

in wonder, straining herself back, increasing the tension as Sean's teeth pulled at her clitoris. "Now, now, *NOW!*"

Her voice rose to a shriek, then meaningless babbles of sound ran from her lips in a torrent as she climaxed once more with frenzied intensity.

Sean released the grip of his teeth, and felt the head of the clitoris throbbing wildly against his lips. Then a shiver ran down his spine as the pantry-door opened and a sharp, frigid voice cut the air.

"So *this* is where you are!"

Still grovelling on the floor, Sean twisted his head and stared at Hermione Simpson.

She was standing in the pantry doorway, white-faced, eyes glittering.

"Did I interrupt you – or had you finished?" she asked in a coldly sarcastic tone. Her eyes flicked down to Sean, focusing on his limp penis – then she glanced at Rosie, first at her face then at her wide-open, soaking vulva.

"Did you enjoy that, Rosie?" Her voice was like ice.

"Ma'am, I... I..." Rosie's face was scarlet.

"Come to my room tonight, Rosie," Hermione's voice was soft but frightening. "You haven't been spanked for a long time –

too long, it would seem." Hermione's tongue flicked out and she touched her lips.

"It's time I whipped that nice, round bottom of yours – you must be getting spoiled."

"But, Ma'am, I…"

"Bring my small riding whip to my bedroom tonight at the usual time," Hermione interrupted. "I shall punish you before you go to bed." Her eyes went onto Sean's face. "It's too bad you can't do these things on your own time, Sean. I don't pay you to suck Rosie off whenever she – or you – gets the urge!"

He stared at his mistress in silence.

Hermione's hand dropped onto her belly, and she massaged herself very slowly. "However, since that's what you enjoy doing, Sean – " she paused, licked her lips again, then said, "Come to my room after I've punished Rosie – and you'll get what you deserve."

She turned, took a step into the kitchen then snapped over her shoulder, "And now that you've finished your fucking – get on with the work I pay you for!"

They listened to her heels tip-tapping across the floor then looked at each other in shocked silence.

Rosie spoke at last. "Cold fish, dirty bitch!" she whispered.

Sean nodded very slowly. His penis moved of its own accord and he gave it a surprised look then encircled it with his hand, squeezed and felt the shaft coming alive, throbbing within his fingers. "She's a bitch all right," he murmured, then added almost inaudibly, "a hungry, fucking bitch!" His cock jerked inside his hand and he tightened the grip of his fingers.

Chapter 3

Alison took her time about dressing for dinner. "There'll be a guest," Rosie Williams had told her, and added, "Mrs. Simpson eats at eight."

She showered, then relaxed on the bed in her bathrobe, and wondered about the sudden spasm of sexuality that had flooded her body when she was undressing and had teased her until she had succumbed to its urging, spread herself on her back on the bed and masturbated to a devastating climax.

"Jonathan!" she murmured to herself. "No more Jonathan!"

She thought about it for a moment, then remembered the beautiful, but sparsely populated, countryside that surrounded Lazonby Hall, and sadly thought to herself, "No more anybody!"

She had got used to the regular sessions of lovemaking that she had enjoyed with Jonathan – and she had enjoyed them, enjoyed them more and more as their affair had progressed – and she wondered now how she would manage without him. Whatever his other shortcomings, Jonathan had been a very satisfying lover.

There was always somebody, she tried to reassure herself, for every hungry girl there was a man – at least one man! But this wasn't busy London, she had to remind herself, this was a remote part of Somerset.

Alison sighed, dragged herself to her feet and started to dress for dinner. She should have considered this aspect of leaving London before. It was a little too late to worry about it now!

"Doctor Maurice Bell," said Hermione Simpson, introducing Alison at the dinner table, "and this is my daughter, Jillian."

Alison was confused. The Doctor appeared to be a rather distinguished-looking individual in his middle forties, she guessed. She turned to shake hands with Jillian first, but she was nowhere to be seen; in her stead there stood an astonishingly handsome youth, a boy of sixteen, perhaps, of medium height and slim build wearing jeans and an open-necked check shirt. His strong, clean-cut features were softened by dark, thick, lustrous hair, cut short, and enormous, heavily-lashed, green eyes, cool and cat-like. But it was his mouth that fascinated Alison: full and sensual, yet with a sardonic cast to it, it was almost girlish in its delicate delineation. And that was when the penny dropped. Girlish – why, this was Jillian! She looked like a beautiful boy, yet... despite the masculine features there was something undeniably feminine about her, too. Recovering herself just in time, she stammered a slightly muted greeting.

"How do you do!"

"Hello, Alison," said Jillian. Her voice had a soft, rather musical quality; she stepped forward to give Alison a handshake that was firm yet slightly lingering. "I'm very pleased to meet you."

"It's a pleasure to meet you, Miss Jeffreys," said Maurice Bell, smoothly; his handshake was gentle and self-assured, but his warm hand also enveloped hers for a fraction of a second longer than seemed absolutely necessary.

He was a handsome man, Alison decided, glancing at the deeply-tanned, slightly saturnine face with its firm lips that now broke into a welcoming smile.

His eyes rested on her face with more than casual interest, and Alison wondered, absently but automatically, whether he was single or married.

* * *

Rosie Williams served dinner with the help of – Alison noticed with surprise – Sean O'Toole.

"There's been a mild epidemic," said Doctor Bell casually, during the course of the meal, "at a village a few miles from here and everybody has to be inoculated against it."

"Epidemic!" Alison sounded alarmed.

Maurice Bell made a depreciatory motion with his hand. "Nothing serious, Miss Jeffreys, I assure you – it's merely an Asian 'flu, very rare for this country – and I've brought the necessary vaccine – "

Hermione Simpson cut in. "I asked Maurice to bring it over for you, Alison, then you could be inoculated like all of us."

Alison blinked, thinking about it. She always hated having any kind of injection – but if everybody else had had them... She gave a small sigh of resignation and murmured, "I just hate having things stuck into me."

Jillian, who had remained silent until now, gave a seemingly unsympathetic little laugh.

She glanced at the slim, beautiful girl-boy, noticing how graceful she seemed, but it occurred to Alison that it was the gracefulness of neither a girl nor a boy, but a young, predatory animal. A leopard or a jaguar, she mused. Her table manners were casual, Alison decided: she ate carelessly with little regard for etiquette, sometimes eating with her mouth slightly open. And yet – it was not an ugly sight; once more, she became acutely aware of Jillian's well-defined, mobile lips. A slight shiver ran down her back – as if she were experiencing some sort of subliminal response to this strange young woman's aura of sensuality.

Jillian became aware of her scrutiny, and she surprised Alison by turning towards her and looking straight back at her with huge, unblinking eyes. Alison quickly glanced away, but not before Jillian had swept her tongue over her upper lip, as if to reclaim a crumb of bread – or did it have some other purpose? Had there been an infinitesimally small change in her expression? A hint of light mockery, perhaps? A piece of bread slipped from her hand, and Jillian bent down in her chair, groping under the table for it.

She was seated opposite her mother, on Alison's left, and after her head had disappeared under the table Alison imagined she felt something brush against the bare thigh-flesh above the top stockings she had donned for dinner.

She started. "Surely she hadn't touched the insides of my legs!" she thought.

There was a look of quiet satisfaction on Jillian's face when her head reappeared.

I must have imagined it, Alison told herself: surely, I must have!

Jillian was the first to finish her soup, and she sat, hands on her lap, waiting for the next course.

Alison became aware that Jillian Simpson was looking at her again; slightly rattled, her napkin slipped from her fingers. She murmured an 'excuse me' then bent under the table to retrieve it. About to straighten up, something caught her eye that made her freeze. Jillian wasn't sitting with her hands in her lap as she had supposed. Her jeans were unbuttoned at the front, her right hand dug deep inside her panties – and busy. She was masturbating – almost openly – at dinner!

Alison raised her head quickly, blood flooding her face then draining out, leaving her cheeks pale and wan. Her soup spoon clattered nervously against the side of her bowl.

"She's like an animal in more ways than one," she thought.

Alison ploughed through the meal mechanically, listening to the conversation between Doctor Bell and Mrs. Simpson with half an ear, and answering absently when she had to. Her mind was on other things... Jillian's relentless, cool gaze and that hand, so busy in her knickers! "Was she... looking at me and playing with herself?" Alison dismissed the thought from her mind almost as soon as it arrived.

She glanced at Jillian's face. She was still staring at her – and her hand had dropped under the table again.

A strange shiver ran through her body. Now I'm convinced: she's definitely playing with herself while she stares at me. Jillian Simpson is a raging lesbian? Surely, she couldn't...?

The thought horrified her, yet at the same time, perversely thrilled her!

It's horrible, she told herself. And I seem to be the object of her lust! Then she wondered, "how would it feel to have another girl touch me in my most intimate places? Probably no worse than a man – in fact they might be a lot better at some things."

Her face grew pink at the idea and she smiled to herself a little. *How could I even think about something as bizarre as that? I must be missing Jonathan more than I thought!*

* * *

"Sure you won't have some wine?" asked Mrs. Simpson.

Alison had declined it before, but this time she changed her mind. "Just a little, please." She drained the glass and didn't demur when Doctor Bell refilled it.

God! After seeing that I deserve a drink! She picked up the fresh glass of wine, and drank it thirstily.

"When the Doctor's given you your vaccination – we'll show you around the manor," said Mrs. Simpson. "It dates back to the sixteenth century; I think you'll find it interesting."

But Alison wasn't listening to the last part of the sentence. She was thinking of the needle and the injection!

"Will... will it hurt?" she asked, nervously.

Maurice Bell's deep, reassuring voice

answered her, "You'll hardly notice it, my dear. Trust me – I pride myself on a completely painless injection."

Gently, he took her elbow and led her to a corner of the room. "Won't take a minute," he told her, taking a needle and syringe from a small black case on the side table.

As usual, Alison turned her head away; first a sharp smell of alcohol as he swabbed her arm – then she was scarcely aware of the tiny prick before he spoke again. "There – that's all there is to it!"

She turned, smiling her relief. "I – I didn't even feel you do it!"

"Just as I said," he smiled, leading her back to Mrs. Simpson.

* * *

There was a small room which Mrs. Simpson used as an office, on the main floor of the manor. "You can rearrange things as you like," Hermione Simpson said. "I'll leave everything up to you – I'm dreadful at office work, anyway."

Alison stared at the desk and papers. It would be kind of nice to have her own place where she could work as much – or as little – as she wanted.

"It all looks very neat," she said,

indicating the big, bare desk and filing cabinets.

Hermione Simpson laughed. "That's because I cleared it up for your benefit, Alison."

As well as the dining-room, there was a large, well-stocked library on the main floor, too, as well as two small oak-panelled sitting rooms and a large drawing-room with an open fireplace. Alison was impressed by the quantity of fine old pictures and antique furniture.

"My husband was an amateur astronomer," said Mrs. Simpson, leading the way up to the top floor of the manor. "He converted this part of the attic into a small observatory."

Alison looked around her with amazement. She'd never seen this kind of a place in a private home before. The mass of telescopes and other optical instruments fascinated her.

She moved towards a large telescope with its own mirror, then staggered. "I'm – I'm feeling rather... rather dizzy," she said uncertainly.

She was vaguely aware of a small, undecipherable sound from Jillian, then Mrs. Simpson took her by the arm into a sort of small, low-ceilinged antechamber to the observatory; there was a single divan but no other furniture. "Why don't you lie down for a moment, Alison dear, while I fetch you a glass of water," she said, sounding solicitous. She lay down gratefully, feeling relieved that she hadn't fainted but a little embarrassed at the trouble she was causing. And then she remembered nothing further.

Dr. Bell gave her another injection.

As the needle plunged into Alison's arm for the second time she lay very still on the simple bed, her eyes open but unseeing, and the voices and sounds in the small room were just a garbled cacophony to her drugged ears.

"That'll keep her pretty much out for four or five hours," said Dr. Bell. "And she won't remember a thing!"

He removed the needle from the syringe, replaced them both in a small case and snapped it shut.

"Thank you, *Doctor* Bell," said Hermione, with ironic emphasis on the 'Doctor': they both knew that Maurice Bell was no longer a doctor, not since a zealous medical association had struck him off because of 'unethical' behaviour – as they viewed his illegal operations and indiscriminate use of prohibited drugs.

"I don't like doing this," the ex-doctor

muttered now, looking at the young girl on the bed.

A tousled lock of dark hair had fallen onto her forehead, making Alison Jeffreys look even younger than her twenty-three years. Her big, brown eyes – usually luminous and alert – were dull and listless, and her five-foot-one, seven stone body slumped, rather than lay, on the bed in the upstairs room in the strange, rambling mansion in a remote part of Somerset.

"You don't have to like it," said Hermione Simpson, coldly. "You just have to do what you're told." She jerked her head toward the door.

"We'll go downstairs now." She turned to the fourth occupant of the room, a forced parody of a smile playing on her lips.

"She's all yours, Jillian, dear." She moved to the bedroom door, opened it, half-pushed Maurice Bell into the corridor, then her smile became a leer as she added to her daughter, "Enjoy yourself, Jillian." Her eyes flickered to the drugged girl again, and she ran a tongue over her lips as she finished in a whisper, "If you need me – just call." Then she moved out of the bedroom quickly, clicking shut the door behind her.

"It... it's wrong," muttered Maurice as

he descended the narrow stairway behind Hermione.

"Don't be ridiculous," she snapped over her shoulder. "It's not wrong at all." She reached the foot of the stairs, and moved toward the old-fashioned but well-furnished sitting-room. "Just because poor Jillian – my daughter, remember – is somewhat attracted to girls it's no reason she should be denied the... the normal pleasures of sexual..." she paused, only to spit out the word, "... intercourse while she's going through this... phase."

"Sexual intercourse!" Maurice repeated, staring at the severe, but still beautiful, forty-five year-old. "She doesn't want sexual intercourse. She wants perverted, unnatural sex!" He moved to a sideboard, poured himself a whiskey from the decanter, then took a big gulp as though he needed it very badly. "That – that freak – she's like a lust-crazed animal. All she wants is..."

"*Don't* call my daughter a freak!" Hermione's voice rose, quivering high with anger. "It's... it's just... just a phase she's going through – and she's just a little 'different' in some ways." She snatched up the gin decanter, poured herself a generous measure, added tonic and ice and then lifted it to her lips.

Maurice watched her, a scornful expression on his dark, still-handsome face. "Listen," he spoke in a low, urgent voice, "if you don't accept that Jillian is a predatory, active lesbian, you're just fooling yourself! Sooner or later you'll have to admit to yourself that the heiress to Lazonby is an out-and-out raving dyke! You can't go on pretending that she's a perfectly conventional, normal girl. Sooner or later the whole county will find out. You'd be far better off letting her go up to London where she'll find more of her sort. There! I've finally said it!" He drained his glass in one gulp.

Naked, Jillian Simpson stared down at the softly curved, lusciously inviting girl on the bed. A dark smile of anticipation crossed her fresh features, and she actually licked her lips as her eyes drank in the sight of young and helpless female flesh that lay at her mercy.

She ran her hands over her slim, well-toned body. Slim but by no means slight, from behind her body might well have been that of a boy, were it not for her flaring hips and her small but decidedly feminine bottom. One hand came to rest upon one of her small, pert breasts and tweaked the nipple into hardness, while the other dived to the base of her flat belly, where a mass of dark hair grew, and started to manipulate the wet, fleshy labia, causing a slight squishing sound.

Her victim was wearing a white cotton blouse and a short, black, pleated skirt; her feet, shoeless now, and legs, were encased in sheer nylons.

Jillian reached to the top of her blouse, unbuttoned it, then gripped the thin fabric of her brassiere. She slipped a hand underneath, unhooked the clasp, and with a firm jerk pulled the undergarment off. Her eyes narrowed as she stared at the twin mounds of soft, fragile flesh – then she began to slowly stroke Alison's breasts.

A low, almost silent laugh came from deep in her throat as she caressed the silky smoothness, letting the puckered texture of the nipples caress the palms of her hands.

Throughout this assault Alison lay unmoving, unseeing, and unaware.

Taking her time, Jillian dropped to her knees beside the bed, pressed her face over the girl's comatose body, encircled a small, pointed, pink nipple with her mouth, and sucked it with a hungry pleasure.

"Mmm, Alison – ohh, Alison," she sighed, sucking and licking with wet, squelching sounds. She drew her head back abruptly, letting the saliva-slicked nipple slide from her lips with a plop. "Mummy's really outshone herself this time," she murmured, and a tight smile of anticipation played over her lips, "she's gone and found me a beauty. A real beauty. And all for me to play with." Her hand dropped down the semi-conscious girl's body to a point just above her skirt. "Mummy said – enjoy yourself – and that's just what I intend to do, girlie!" Her smile became wider. "And I can enjoy myself in any way I please." With this, she reached down still further to the hem of her skirt and pulled it up, feasting her eyes on the sight that met her avid gaze.

Alison's panties stretched tightly over her belly and hips, so thin that the dark triangle of her pubic hairs was clearly visible. Jillian tore at the flimsy garment with both hands, ripping the fragile silk, exposing the dark mound between her smoothly fleshed thighs.

Jillian's eyes fastened on the thatch of dark foliage, then she touched it, stroking it tentatively, gently at first, then with mounting urgency. Her hand travelled lower still, probing between the exposed thighs, and found vaginal lips that were soft and moist. She felt inside them.

"Mmmm! Nice pussy," she purred, rubbing her finger between Alison's increasingly juicy labia. "Soft and wet, just like a pussy should be!"

She stretched out a strong arm, gripped one of Alison's feet, and moved it toward the side of the bed – then did the same with her other foot.

The silk-encased legs formed a gleaming V to the ruined briefs that flapped open at the crotch. Jillian panted as she stared up into the wet pinkness. "Fuck," she groaned under her breath.

She climbed over the end of the bed, breathing heavily, and crawled between the outstretched legs. Her taut, muscular thighs pressed against Alison's soft silkiness. She started to kiss her way down, down, down towards the wet, waiting opening.

Her breath mingled with Alison's as she lay face to face on top of the girl, now as still as a corpse.

She reached under her body again, with both hands this time, and gripped Alison's thighs, spreading them apart into an agonising, strained split. "I'm going to fuck you now, my darling," she half-moaned as she felt Alison's wet cunt and the soft curls above it brush against her belly. "I'm going to fuck you as you've never been fucked in your life!"

Jillian leapt from the bed and went over to a chest of drawers. She opened a drawer and removed a strange contraption of rubber and leather – and a little jug of thick, whitish liquid. After she had completed the necessary adjustments, she pulled on the strap-on double dildo, carefully inserting one end into her sopping vagina so that the other stood out and upwards from her groin, astonishingly like a real male penis. Indeed, in the soft, dim light of the little room, a casual observer could be forgiven for assuming that this was a man about to ravish the girl who lay so peacefully and so still on the divan in front of him.

The strange girl-boy now knelt between Alison's thighs and, holding the black rubber dildo with one hand, gently parted the lips of Alison's cunt with the other. She ran the tip of the stiff phallus up and down the cleft of the older girl's sex, eliciting a vague moan of pleasure from her.

"So you like that, do you, little secretary-girl? Well, how about this?" And she cruelly thrust the shaped head of the phallus several inches into Alison's cunt, making her moan loudly with unequivocal satisfaction.

She drove herself inward, causing the stretched vaginal walls to be forced open even more widely. Alison's body jerked upward as she thrust the huge phallus into the near-unconscious girl. She pressed her face onto Alison's, groping for her soft mouth

with her own firm, feverish lips, kissing her with a furious, naked hunger.

She screwed her dildo in and out with ever-increasing strength and speed. Alison's body had become a jerking mass of tortured flesh as her assailant's climax began.

"Squirt…" she screamed suddenly, "I'm going to squirt my stuff inside you – just like all those filthy boys do!" She dragged in a gasp of air as her own vagina contracted and then expanded. "Right inside your pussy – so hot, so wet…" she babbled as the crest of her climax neared. "*Aaaargh!*" She let out a deep groan then writhed her body wildly. She reached down to squeeze the bulb of the curious contraption between her thighs. And as she squeezed convulsively, the little hole in the rounded head of her dildo opened, emitting a searing spurt of thick, warm cream, then closed – then opened again, spurting again deep into Alison Jeffreys' cunt. "Oooohhh yesss! Fuck – I'm fucking your hot little cunt!" Her voice went high, and then racking tremors shook her body as she squeezed out the last squirts of liquid.

She fell back and the long black dildo pulled out of Alison's battered pussy with an obscene sucking noise.

Jillian Simpson lay on top of Alison, breathing deeply, languorous with satiation.

"That was nice. Very nice," she mumbled, licking at Alison's face. "What a lovely soft cunt you have, my darling Alison! Mmmm!" She sniffed her fingers appreciatively. "And it smells delicious, too!"

She squirmed herself down to the foot of the bed, and stared in between her victim's legs, grotesquely stretched open, and started to lick the oozing, swollen vulva like a madwoman. She took a mouthful of the thick, whitish cream that she had squirted through the dildo into Alison's vagina at the moment of her climax, lifted her head and swallowed deeply. Savouring the exotic mix of the dairy cream and Alison's own thick vaginal secretions, she went back to her task, taking each of the unconscious girl's swollen inner sex lips in her mouth, one at a time, and gently worrying it with her teeth and massaging it with a busy tongue.

"Tastes good, too!"

She smiled, as though she'd performed a clever feat. As she licked and sucked at the juicy vulva, she stroked the insides of Alison's thighs, then parted and lifted her bottom-cheeks to reveal the tight pucker of her nut-brown anus.

Jillian let her tongue slide less than an inch further down until she felt the wrinkled skin of Alison's arsehole. She gave the puckered orifice a brief licking, noting with interest that her victim squirmed sensuously when she did this. Hmm, she thought, there's something there that can wait for another time, perhaps.

She guided the stiff shaft to the vaginal entrance once more. This time it was easier; Alison's vulva was still flaring open from the previous onslaught of the huge artificial penis – it slid in smoothly, sensuously, stretching the abused and fragile flesh without effort.

Jillian grunted in satisfaction.

* * *

Downstairs in the sitting-room, Maurice Bell slammed down his glass. "D'you realise what time it is?" he snapped to Hermione. "She's been up there with that – that poor kid – for four hours!"

Hermione didn't even glance up from the book she was reading.

Maurice leaned forward, and spoke urgently. "It's midnight." He tapped the face of his watch. "That stuff'll be wearing off soon!"

Hermione looked up this time. "Oh, Maurice – let the poor girl have her fun!"

"Fun!" Maurice looked startled then

angry. "D'you call raping a young, drugged girl fun?"

Hermione snapped shut her book. "Don't act so bloody righteous." She paused, then went on, "After what I know about you…"

"Don't go into all that again…" he muttered.

She gave him a sharp, humourless smile. "If I *did* go into that, there'd be criminal proceedings against you – not just being struck off – "

"I said – don't go into that," said Maurice, more loudly. He took a deep breath. "As I just said – that stuff'll be wearing off."

"What was it anyway?" asked Hermione curiously. "Just what exotic solution did you inject into that girl?"

"Exotic is right," he muttered. "It's some stuff they use in the Far East when someone's in agonising pain – it dulls everything – deadens the nerves – "

"Some herbal remedy – " Hermione's voice was disdainful.

"Hardly that," Maurice said. "It's strong – can be deadly – stuff."

"But it just lasts four or five hours?"

"Depends on the dosage," he murmured. "That's all I gave her." He glanced at his watch again. "By God – isn't that long enough for that damned daughter of yours to do her thing?"

"Don't blame her," said Hermione. "She's just – just a normal, developing adolescent – with natural instincts." She dropped her eyes as she spoke.

"Normal! Natural!" Maurice gave a mocking laugh, then stopped suddenly. "You'd better go and drag your 'normal' daughter off her latest victim!"

Hermione glared at Maurice angrily, then got to her feet. "I suppose I'd better go up." She smoothed down her skirt. "You and Jillian'll have to carry her back to her room before she comes to – it wouldn't do to have her come round in the attic!"

"Is that what you got her out here for," asked Maurice, "so that your daughter could rape her, abuse her and amuse herself with her body?"

"No!" Hermione spoke emphatically. "I really needed a secretary – that's why I advertised!"

Maurice shook his head in anger and despair as Hermione swept from the room.

Chapter 4

Alison started to regain consciousness very slowly. She was lying on her back and there was a great weight pressing down on her body.

Where am I? she asked herself hazily. What kind of a dream is this?

She tried to move but something... someone... on top of her prevented it; she realised then that her legs were apart – she was wide open; something moving on top of her, a hand between her legs, and... she shivered: There's something trying to get INSIDE ME! Alison attempted to turn – but couldn't. It's coming right into my pussy – filling me like I've never been filled! She tried to struggle frantically but the solid shaft pinned her to the bed as though she were a butterfly.

The huge column inside her vulva churned upward and Alison could feel her vagina being stretched and strained wider and wider open. Oh, my God – what's happening?

The gross rod slid further in and the walls of Alison's vagina undulated against it. It's fucking me! *A monstrous cock is fucking my pussy!*

She tried to open her eyes but all she could see was a red haze. Am I dreaming? Is this real? A thrill ran through her belly as the massive organ pressed against her clitoris. I'm having a dream – a thrilling sex-dream that's going to make me come!

She gave up the effort of trying to understand, let her eyelids drop, shut out the red haze – then the thrills came again, more strongly.

The huge snake in her pussy was squirming wildly, pressing against many different parts of her vulva simultaneously. The tip of her clitoris was dragged inward by the thrust of the giant cock and as the shaft writhed, fierce throbs of ecstasy rocked through her sexual flesh. She felt the air panting from her lungs and her breasts, flattened against the mass of flesh on top of her, ached when she tried to move them. Her body jerked up the bed as the rod drove in deep again; she could feel wetness seeping out of her pussy, trickling down the sides of her distended labia then wetting the tops of her thighs each time the cock pulled out.

A violent jolt of pleasure shot up to the top of her belly and she groaned and drew in her pelvis – making the cock press more strongly against her clitoris. I'm going to come – I've never felt like this! This dream is the most – the wildest – I'm *coming*!

Her clitoris was a crazy bobbing spire of sexuality as she started a wild orgasm. Right from my clit to my pussy – then round to my bottom and more – I'm coming all over!

Alison's lips opened in a soundless scream; she arrived at her orgasm again and again, jerking her thighs and feeling her vaginal lips closing, squeezing down on the alien snake that was fucking her with such relentless energy.

It's going right through the front door and out of the back! I've never been fucked like this – not in a dream or for real!

Jillian made a high, whining, animal-like sound as her orgasm started again. The hot juice flowed from her cunt in ragged, uneven squirts – flooding over the unconscious girl's already soaking fleece, adding to her own, abundant juices that flooded her engorged sex.

I'm all wet inside! I'm coming and I'm all wet and hot inside my pussy!

The violence of Alison's orgasm increased; a damp sweat covered all parts of her skin. She wanted to cry out squirm herself frantically but felt as though she was still in the grip of a dream. The sexual spasms became unbearably intense as her orgasm reached an impossible peak – then the limits of Alison's endurance were passed, and she dropped into unconsciousness again.

* * *

Jillian was still lying on top of the unconscious girl, her double-ended rubber dildo sliding slowly from their saturated pussies, when Hermione and Maurice came to the bedroom door.

"Still doing her thing!" Maurice muttered angrily when he saw the position of the figures on the bed.

He hurried over to Alison's side, then reached down and drew up her eyelid. "Still unconscious," he murmured to himself, then added, "Poor girl!"

"Don't waste your time feeling sorry for her," said Hermione coldly. "She doesn't know what's happening – and would probably enjoy it if she did." She spoke to her daughter. "Jillian, dear – get off her now. It's time to stop; you can play with her again tomorrow!"

Jillian turned a dazed face towards her mother, and then gave a weary grin.

"She's a bloody good fuck, Mummy – I had her twice!"

"Yes, dear," said Hermione. "You

certainly did! Now get off her – it's getting late."

Reluctantly, Jillian squirmed herself to the foot of the bed, her dildo dangling limply in her hand. She brought it up and waved it under her mother's nose and smiled.

"I did it twice, Mummy – I fucked her sweet cunt twice!"

"Yes, quite so, dear," said Hermione again. "Now get dressed and come downstairs."

Maurice listened to the conversation with an expression of distaste on his face. When Jillian had dragged on her trousers and shirt, then let her doting mother lead her from the room, Maurice turned his attention to Alison again.

She was lying very still, eyes closed, lips parted as she breathed deeply through her nose.

Absently, Maurice stroked her cheeks. She was still, gave no sign of awareness. He noticed her breasts, touched the pink tips very gently and a tender smile crossed his face.

"You've got virginal breasts, Alison," he murmured, "but you're certainly no virgin!"

As he spoke, his eyes moved down her body, stopping at the top of her thighs. Her legs were still stretched open and the insides of her thighs were sopping wet. Maurice bent, staring into her vagina. It was swollen and open, making a wide, pink sexual mouth, which oozed a semi-opaque, creamy fluid.

Maurice touched it with a fingertip, sliding his finger on the edges of wet flesh. "Poor little pussy," he whispered. "You've been well fucked – *too* bloody well fucked!"

He touched the clitoris, and Alison flinched. "So aware!" he murmured.

His face became excited. "I must examine you – fully and completely – and test you!" He thrust his finger deep inside her vaginal tunnel, savouring the feel of warm, wet sensuality. "You must come to my office tomorrow, Alison, my girl."

Then Maurice stooped, lifted Alison in his arms and carefully carried her downstairs to her bedroom.

She was still unconscious when he placed her on her bed. He stripped off her shredded panties then dampened a towel in the washbasin and wiped the outside, then inside, of her vagina.

She submitted to his ministrations without a sign of life. Maurice searched among her clothes until he found a short nightie, which he took to her bed. Carefully, he removed her torn brassiere and blouse then slipped the nightie over her head.

He had scarcely completed his task when Alison's eyelids flickered, then opened. A small frown of puzzlement creased her forehead.

"Where am I?" she blinked at Maurice.

He sank onto the edge of her bed. "You're all right, Alison – you're at Lazonby Hall."

Alison sighed, remembering. "But what's happened? Why am I here in bed?"

She looked down at herself in surprise.

"You fainted, Alison," Maurice said smoothly, "it happens that way sometimes, after a shot – you remember the shot I gave you?"

She nodded slowly. "Yes, I remember."

"There's nothing wrong. You'll feel fine in the morning; just have a good sleep – then in the afternoon, come and see me at my office." He pulled a card from his pocket, thrust it into her hand; then took it back, placed it on her bedside table. "You're all right, Alison, but I want to examine you – make a few tests."

Alison nodded again; a dream expression on her face, then she reached under the bedclothes and he saw her cheeks get red.

"What is it?" he asked, quietly.

She lowered her eyes, then whispered. "I – I was dreaming."

He nodded.

She opened her eyes wide. "An – an awful kind of dream."

"What, Alison?"

"You're a doctor," she said. "I can talk to you?"

He nodded again.

"It – it was like – like a sex dream," she whispered, flushing. "I – I dreamed that – that – " she broke off, looking embarrassed.

"Dreamed you were with a man?" Maurice prompted.

She nodded her head eagerly. "Yes. Isn't that awful?"

"It's quite normal. Did you have an orgasm?"

"Yesss – " she groaned. "Oh, did I *ever*!"

"That should relax you, Alison. You'll sleep well tonight."

Her hand moved under the covers, then she met Maurice's eyes with a puzzled expression. "But – but I feel as though I've really had a man inside me, I'm all... open, you know what I mean?"

Her face was flushed.

"Dreams can be very vivid," Maurice reassured her.

"I – I'm sore down there – Doctor, my pussy's all sore as though I've had a – a big thing inside me!" Her voice was a whisper.

"But you don't hurt?" he asked.

"Not hurt – but sore and..." She hesitated.

"Aroused?" he asked.

Her flush became deeper, and then she nodded. He saw her hand move under the covers.

"Do you masturbate Alison?" he asked quietly.

She bit at her lips, closed her eyes.

"Do you?" he persisted.

Alison didn't answer.

Suddenly, Maurice whipped the sheets down. Alison was lying with her thighs slightly parted and her hand was over her crotch. Two fingers had spread open her vaginal lips and a third finger was pressing on the head of her clitoris.

"Just sometimes," she whispered.

"That's normal," Maurice said. "You should make yourself come whenever you feel like it – it'll relax you."

"Yes," she nodded eagerly, "it always relaxes me – helps me to go to sleep."

"If you feel like it – do it," he said.

"Yes," she said, her eyes still closed, cheeks still red.

Maurice took a small vial from his pocket and shook out a pill.

"If you find it hard to sleep tonight – take one of these." He placed the pill beside his card on her bedside table.

"Thank you, Doctor."

"Will you be all right now?"

"I think so." She opened her eyes, smiled at Maurice then pulled up the sheets over her nakedness.

Maurice smiled at her, and then stroked her face very gently. "You're a very pretty girl, Alison. I hope I'll see a lot of you while you're here."

"Yes," she said, smiling back.

"Comfortable?" He slid his hand under the covers; he let it glide down her body to the soft, warm flesh of her thighs.

She flinched pressed her legs together and when his hand went near her crotch; then he took his hand away.

"Remember what I said – if you can't go to sleep."

"You mean?" Her eyebrows were raised.

He smiled and got to his feet. "You can take the pill – or make yourself come – or both."

Alison gave a nervous laugh. "No doctor's ever told me to do that before."

Maurice laughed back. "But then you've never met a doctor like me, my dear!"

"I mean it," he said. He moved toward the door, then said over his shoulder, "Don't forget to come and see me at my office tomorrow afternoon."

"If Mrs. Simpson doesn't need me!"

"Don't worry about that. I'll tell her."

"Good night, doctor."

"Good night, Alison," he answered, exiting.

Chapter 5

The smooth, voluptuous half-moons of Rosie's buttocks stared into Hermione's face as the cook positioned herself over the back of the low chair.

Hermione's eyes glittered and her tongue snaked out to moisten her dry lips. She was wearing a leather skirt which was so brief that Rosie had caught a glimpse of dark pubic hair at Hermione's crotch each time the mistress of Lazonby moved. The halter was leather, too: a thin strip that barely concealed the firm, shapely, but not over-large, breasts. Her breasts rose now, as Hermione drew in a deep breath.

"You deserve to be disciplined, don't you, Rosie?" Hermione hissed.

Rosie nodded her head. From past experience she knew better than to speak. All that Hermione wanted from her was obedience – and the use of her firm, naked flesh upon which to vent her weird, sadistic obsession.

When she had entered Hermione's bedroom, her mistress had indicated to her the familiar chair and straight-away Rosie had bent over it, exposing her bare bottom and stocking-less thighs for her employer's delectation.

Hermione toyed with the short whip that Rosie had obediently brought her, moved closer to the waiting flesh, then snapped: "Open your thighs more, Rosie – let me see that precious quim that you so adore having sucked. Bend your knees; relax, my dear; enjoy what I'm going to do!"

Rosie stifled a moan, forced her legs to relax and let her thighs part. A trickle of moistness escaped from her labia and ran down the inside of her thigh.

Hermione stooped, gazing into the cook's pink slit. Rosie's vaginal lips were still swollen and spread out as though they had not fully recovered from the battering they had received in the pantry. Hermione looked into them, then reversed her grip on the whip and attempted to slide the specially rounded end of the handle into Rosie's vagina.

Rosie flinched, instinctively tightening the

cheeks of her bottom, gripping the end of the handle, preventing it from entering her.

Hermione jerked the whip angrily. "Relax, Rosie – don't try and stop me!"

A bubble of fear seemed to ooze from Rosie's lips. "Don't hurt, Ma'am – please don't hurt me!"

"Relax your legs and your bottom," Hermione hissed, "or I'll give you such pain as you'll never forget!"

Shivers of fear ran across Rosie's flesh; then her buttocks grew limp and opened – and Hermione drove the phallic handle of the whip into her cook's cunt.

"Now, isn't that nice?" said Hermione *sotto voce* as she drove the two-inch wide whip handle between the vaginal lips.

Rosie took short, jerky breaths as the leather 'phallus' penetrated her.

Hermione squirmed around the whip's butt-end, watching the wet flesh clutch at it, oozing out when she pulled down, dragging in when she inserted it more deeply. Her hand went to the front of her short skirt and she reached under it, caressing herself as she watched the pulsating genitals.

"You've got a big, wet cunt, Rosie – " Hermione purred. "D'you like having it fucked?" She jerked the leather butt in deeply.

Rosie could feel herself being pressed against the back of the chair as the whip-end went in. "Y-yes, Ma'am," was all she could gasp.

Hermione turned her weapon, twisted it until it was squashed against Rosie's clitoris. She saw the cook become tense.

"You like having your pussy sucked off, don't you, Rosie?" Hermione tormented.

"Uuuuh, yes – aah, yes, Ma'am!" Rosie whimpered. The leather butt was titillating her clitoris, bringing on early thrills.

"You like what I'm doing?" Hermione asked in a whisper.

She pressed the leather gently against the head of the clitoris, dragging it down and pushing it up with careful, skilful movements.

Rosie arched her back, savouring the delicious pleasure of hard leather caressing her most vulnerable parts. "Y-yes, Ma'am!" she panted, rotating her buttocks gently in cadence with the turns of the butt.

Hermione's eyes glittered more wildly. Suddenly, she withdrew the butt-end, reversed her grip – and then brought the thong down on Rosie's writhing, waiting buttocks with all her strength.

The sound of the lash echoed around the bedroom.

"Aiee! Ma'am, you're cutting me!"

Rosie's frenzied squeal blended with the sound of whipped flesh as Hermione slashed down again.

Two red lines appeared on the fleshy buttocks; Hermione watched them turn white, then red again and she squeezed her thighs together and rocked herself back and forward, tightly and tensely, as though she herself was experiencing great excitement. Her hand rose again and the whip slashed down, cutting the skin, drawing a streak of blood from the victim's bottom. Rosie squealed again and the sound seemed to increase Hermione's excitement; she rocked herself more quickly as she rained down a welter of blows on the helpless cook's bottom.

Rosie's squeals had changed into a frightened whining sound. She was flattened on the chair back, buttocks protruding obediently, flinching at each slash, and a stream of yellow urine was trickling from her vulva and forming a small pool on the carpet.

Hermione gave an extra hard slap and, noticing the little puddle between the cook's feet, taunted, "You can't hold your water, Rosie – you never could hold your water. Take *that* – " she slashed down with all her strength, "for soiling my beautiful carpet, you disgusting slut – and *that*!" The whip lashed down again and Rosie's bottom became a quivering mass of tortured flesh.

Hermione stopped her punishment as abruptly as she'd started it. She stepped back and leaned against the end of her bed, breathing deeply through her nose. "Get out, Rosie – I'm through with you."

The cook straightened herself painfully, letting her skirt drop into place, then reaching under it, caressed her striped buttocks tenderly.

Hermione smiled into her tear-streaked face. "Hurt, Rosie?"

Rosie nodded, and swallowed the lump in her throat.

"You'd rather have your cunt sucked, eh?" The crude words were vicious and as she spoke Hermione dragged up the front of her skirt, exposing an unexpectedly dense pubic bush and ruddy, swollen lips below. She inserted a fingertip between them, probing inside her as she went on talking.

"I'm sorry, but that's all you'll get for now, Rosie – for now – " She laughed, a little too high. "But never mind. There's always a next time, isn't there, Rosie?"

She watched Rosie limp towards the bedroom door, then as she was leaving, Hermione raised her voice and called, "Come in, Sean – it's your turn now!"

Sean, ashen-faced, shambled into the bedroom. He kept his face averted from Rosie as he passed her in the doorway.

"Close the door," said Hermione in a different kind of voice.

He obeyed her, and then stood very still, waiting.

"Rosie must have enjoyed what you were doing to her in the pantry this afternoon," said Hermione quietly, watching Sean's face as she continued to slide her fingertip up and down her sopping sexual cleft.

Sean didn't answer.

Hermione walked to her bed and sat down on the edge, still pleasuring herself. "Whipping Rosie always excites me, Sean," she said in an ordinary tone of voice. "Makes me feel all... hot and bothered – worked up – aroused."

He said nothing, just watched her, warily.

Hermione let her head drop back onto the bed, lifted her feet and propped her heels on the edge. Her knees fell apart and the vivid pink maw of her vulva was exposed to Sean's eyes.

The whip dropped from her hand, then she reached to her vulva, using both hands to spread open the lips so that Sean could see the livid, pearl-like bead of her clitoris slip from under its hood.

"Suck me off, Sean – suck my pussy and make me orgasm with your tongue, your mouth and... use your teeth. You know how I like you to do it!" Her clipped, upper-class tones were strangely at odds with what she was saying and the view of her body that she presented to him.

Slowly, Sean moved forward on leaden feet.

"Do it well, Sean," said Hermione as he dropped to his knees at the side of the bed, "and maybe I won't beat you so hard – after!"

He thrust his head forward, clamped his lips on the wet, delicately salty flesh of her labia, sucked it into his mouth, chewed on it, squeezed it between his lips then tongued it expertly, searching for and finding her clitoris then drawing it into his mouth and caressing it with his tongue and nibbling it gently with his teeth.

"You do this so well, Sean," purred Hermione, writhing herself with pleasure. "I think that this is the real reason I employ – and pay you – so bloody well!"

He pulled the slender stem with his lips, drawing it as far inside his mouth as he was able, then closed his teeth on it, holding it so that he could titillate the very tip of her clitoris with his tongue.

"Oh God, yes, Sean – marvellous!" Hermione drooled.

She raised and lowered her buttocks very slowly, savouring every delicious thrill.

"Drive your fingers in and out of my pussy while you suck me," she whispered.

She lifted her pelvis to accommodate him, and he reached up with his hand, held two fingers together and drove them into her moist slit.

"Oh, that's good!" Hermione mumbled ecstatically. "Oh, yes... do it harder... deeper!"

She used her heels to lift and lower her pelvis, letting his fingers drive into her more deeply. Her belly tensed and relaxed spasmodically as her sex responded and Sean's mouth became filled with a wet mass of pulsating, churning flesh.

"This – this is – is heaven!" Hermione panted. She was moving herself closer and closer to the edge of the bed, walking herself on her buttocks like feet, making her knees push up higher, thighs parted wider.

"Oh, now, Sean – now!" Hermione's voice was ragged as her orgasm began. Her body jerked, her shoulders lifted and smashed down on the bed, then she was closer and closer to the edge. "Oh, Sean – I'm com... *I'm coming*!" She almost screamed, jerking herself forward, pressing her crotch against Sean's mouth until he leaned backwards, more and more until his balance was lost and Hermione fell on top of him, her vulva still twitching in spasms, clamped to his mouth, as Sean fell onto his back.

The orgasms drained out of her; Hermione slumped forward, thighs gripping Sean's cheeks as his lips still chewed, tiredly, on her sexual flesh.

A long sigh escaped from Hermione's lips. "So good, Sean, so bloody good!"

She started to drag herself to her feet, separating her cunt from his mouth with a wet, squishy sound.

"Stay where you are, Sean," she murmured. "Just unfasten your pants and lie on your face – I'll strap you where you lie."

Her legs were shaky as she stood up, and her hand trembled when she picked up the whip off the bed.

Sean's trousers were halfway down his hips when Hermione turned around.

"Quicker!" she snapped with a sudden change of mood. "Don't make me wait when I want to strap you!"

Sean was half turned over when she slashed down. The vicious blow, delivered through a red haze of lust and desire, missed its target and snapped against Sean's neck.

He made a low sound, then dropped onto his side, unconscious.

Hermione stared at him blankly, then shook her head as though to clear a fog away. "Sean," she murmured, dropping the whip then crouching down beside him, "what have I done?"

Anxiously, she felt at his pulse, then let out her breath in relief.

"You're all right, Sean – " She gave a nervous giggle of relief. "I just knocked you out, that's all!"

He had rolled onto his back and she stared at the dragged-down trousers and the flesh of his belly and thighs. The matted tangle of pubic hair was clearly visible, and below it, like an awakening snake, his penis dangled.

Hermione's expression changed as she stared at it. Slowly, her hand moved and she cupped the large balls that hung in their warm, wrinkled scrotum below the shaft. The organ began to move, becoming thicker, longer. Hermione squeezed the balls; Sean's cock twitched.

She drew in her breath, wetted her lips as though she were hungry or thirsty, then gripped the shaft at the base, encircling the round thickness with a finger and thumb.

Hermione's lips parted, she wetted them

again, and then lowered her head until she was over Sean's abdomen. Her finger and thumb squeezed, the cock swelled and her face went lower until she could suck the organ into her mouth.

With her lips clamped on the shaft of the cock, Hermione changed her position, straddling Sean, her pelvis over his head. She let her weight go down on him, her belly on his chest, her thighs on either side of his face and her pussy inches away from his open mouth.

She pushed his trousers lower then again cupped his balls with her hands, and sucked the smooth cock more deeply into her mouth, slithering her tongue over the tightly stretched skin on the sides, onto the rounded head and tickling the little hole in the tip with the end of her tongue. Sean made a small sound.

Hermione opened her mouth wider, letting her lips slide down the shiny sexual shaft. She could feel small pulses beating beneath the skin. There was salt mixed with the musky, male taste of his organ. She sucked with sensuous pleasure.

Sean groaned and opened his eyes.

Hermione lifted her lips off his cock, then reached down with her mouth, and licked the whole length of his penis. It reared and jerked.

Sean could see his fragrant mistress' vulva close in front of his eyes; he groaned again and felt his confusion lifting.

She made small nipping caresses with her teeth down the entire length of his cock, then she encircled it with her mouth again, gliding her lips over the rounded head, then moving her face up and down as she sucked it like a lollipop.

Sean closed his eyes at the thrilling sensation; this was pure delight. He opened his eyes again, saw Hermione's vulva just inches away and reached for her buttocks, scrabbling at her flesh as he tried to draw her closer to his face.

She felt the movement, sucked his cock more strongly, then wriggled her pelvis back so that it was poised over his mouth.

Sean parted his lips, letting the wide-open cunt squash down onto his lips. It was wet, warm and palpitating. He gently sucked the mass of flesh into his mouth.

Hermione's lips became more insistent, more thrilling, more sensuous. Sean's penis had swollen into a stiff shaft of sex-aroused, blood-engorged flesh; each time her tongue flicked at the head of it, the whole organ jerked.

Suddenly, Sean's entire body stiffened; Hermione heard him dragging in breath with wet, sexy sounds as he kept his lips glued onto her vulva. His pelvis jerked up, and she felt his shaft expand in her mouth. For a second it was very still – then hot spurts squirted from the lips, hitting the back of her throat, scalding it and making her gag as she swallowed frantically, sucking every last drop of sex-juice out of the spitting organ and tasting it with her tongue before she swallowed and felt the tangy fluid dribbling down her throat.

His lips fell off her vulva, and she heard him sucking in air. She rested her face on his thighs, feeling his cock resting against her cheek and softening every second.

"Ohh, Ma'am," said Sean, weakly, "so bloody good – that was the best!"

She turned her head and looked at him as he lay prostrated on his back. A smile fringed her lips, and when she spoke, there was a ring of gooey white sperm all around the edges of her mouth.

"Not all the things I do are bad."

He gave her a tired smile. "Some of them, but not all!" he sighed. "It was so bloody good – so fucking good, Ma'am!" He closed his eyes as though reliving the ecstasy.

She turned herself, crawled up to his face, then bent her head and kissed him on the lips, twisting her tongue in his mouth.

"You taste that?" she asked. "That's your

come-stuff. I'm giving it back to you, Sean – your own fucking spunk!"

"It tastes good," he muttered. "You taste good – even if you are a sadistic bitch!"

Hermione looked angry for a moment, then she laughed.

"Why'd'you have to knock me out?" He massaged the side of his neck tenderly.

She laughed again. "You won't believe it, but it was an accident!"

He shook his head in disbelief.

"But what I did afterward was nice," she murmured.

"Yeah," he sighed, "damned nice!"

"You want to do it again that way – or d'you want to fuck – just plain old fuck?"

He made a wry face, then: "Any way you say, Ma'am – any little thing you want, just say it. You're my fucking mistress!"

She pulled him on top of her, opening her legs so that he fell in between.

His mouth went onto hers again, and she kissed him back as sensuously as he had kissed her. He felt his penis reviving and he steered it into her soaking-wet pussy.

She jerked her mouth off his and spoke. "Too bloody right I'm your mistress, and don't you bloody well forget it!" And she pressed her hungry pussy up to meet the thrust of his stiffening cock.

Chapter 6

Mrs. Simpson had been explaining Alison's duties to her; now they were sitting in the small office where Alison would do most of her work, when Rosie Williams tapped at the door then entered.

"Would you like your coffee in here, Ma'am?" she asked in a subdued voice.

"Yes," said Hermione, then asked, "would you like a coffee, too?"

Alison nodded, glancing at her watch. It was eleven o'clock on her second day – and first morning at Lazonby. Doctor Bell wanted to see her that afternoon, she remembered.

"I'll tell Rosie to bring you coffee every morning at this time if you'd like it," said Hermione.

"That would be nice," said Alison. The cook had looked different from the day before, she thought idly. Her eyes were red-rimmed as though she'd been crying, and she walked slowly, painfully, as though she'd been hurt.

"Is – is she all right?" she asked now hesitantly, wondering if she was being too forward.

Hermione raised her eyebrows and asked, "Rosie?"

Alison nodded. "She – she looks, well, different."

Hermione looked at Alison thoughtfully before she answered. "She was disciplined last night."

Alison showed her surprise. "Disciplined?"

Hermione smiled. "I'm very old-fashioned, Alison. If any of my employees misbehave, I prefer to punish them – rather than discharge them."

Alison stared blankly at her employer.

"Don't you think that's better?" Hermione said smoothly. "I pay very well and I'm sure my employees would prefer trivial discipline rather than losing their jobs."

"How – how do you punish them?" Alison asked in a low voice.

Hermione laughed lightly. "It depends upon the occasion." Her eyes flickered over Alison's shapely figure. "Have you ever been spanked?"

Alison flushed, then murmured, "Only when I was small.

Hermione nodded. "It didn't hurt much, did it? A few light spanks on the bottom don't hurt anyone – and can do a lot of good. They make you aware of your mistake and remind you not to make the same error again."

Alison looked confused. "I – I don't know – " she murmured.

"I'm sure you're very conscientious," said Hermione, "but just supposing you neglected your work for no good reason, wouldn't you prefer to have a few light slaps on your bare bottom instead of being discharged and having the headache of finding another job?"

Alison gave a nervous laugh. "I – I've never thought about it," she admitted. "I don't know how I'd feel!"

Rosie tapped at the door then and entered with two cups of coffee on a tray.

Hermione patted Alison's hand. "Then don't worry your pretty little head thinking about it now; it'll probably never be necessary. D'you like sugar in your coffee?"

"Yes, please," said Alison absently, still seeing an image of herself lying face down on Mrs. Simpson's lap and the woman's hand slapping down on her exposed, naked bottom. Or would she use a strap or a cane? Her cheeks flushed at the thought, and then to her own surprise, she felt a flicker of sexual excitement. How would it feel to expose my soft, sensitive bottom to the eyes of this frightening but fascinating woman?

It has been so long since my daddy

spanked me... How had it felt? How would it feel?

"You're not drinking your coffee," said Hermione.

Alison's flush deepened then she picked up her coffee and sipped at it.

"Not worrying about anything, I hope," said Hermione.

Alison set down her cup, smiling as brightly as she could. "Why no, Mrs. Simpson, nothing at all."

"If you have any problems – any kind of problems – I hope you'll confide in me," said Hermione. "I'm always ready to help my staff." She smiled, sipped her coffee, then added, "I may seem a bit of an old battleaxe to you, but I'm very loyal to my staff as long as they're loyal to me."

"No problems so far," said Alison cheerfully, then she added, "Oh, I've just remembered, Doctor Bell wants to see me this afternoon – will it be all right if I take time off?"

"Of course. The Doctor mentioned it to me last night." Hermione gave Alison a searching look. "Just what does he want to see you for?"

Alison shrugged. "I don't know; some kind of tests, he said."

Hermione drew in her breath. "I see – the tests – it had to be the tests."

She gave a sharp laugh. "Is something wrong?" Alison looked up.

"No, nothing's wrong, Alison," said Hermione, rising to her feet. "It'll be quite all right for you to take the afternoon off and visit my dear friend, Doctor Bell." She moved to the door, then said over her shoulder, "I think two o'clock would be the best time – you know where he lives?"

"He gave me his card."

"I'll have Sean drive you over in the Bentley – be ready right after lunch," said Hermione, leaving the room.

* * *

The big car was waiting outside the manor when Alison ran down the front steps. Lunch, with Mrs. Simpson and Jillian, had been a very quiet affair. The handsome young girl had kept her eyes fixed on her all through the meal, giving rather desultory replies when her mother asked her a question. Like the night before, she had kept playing with herself under the table until Alison – consumed by a horrible curiosity – had deliberately dropped her napkin, bent to retrieve it and taken the chance to stare under the table. With an effort, she had restrained a gasp. Jillian's trousers were open again, and her fingers busy at work – she was so close that Alison could see the juicy labia opening and closing as she caressed them obscenely only inches away.

When she straightened herself, Alison's cheeks were pale. The very audacity of the girl! She swallowed some food with an effort. The image of what she had just seen kept returning to torment her. Why? She thought. She worried that perhaps her desires were beginning to get the better of her!

Colour came back into Alison's cheeks as she remembered her sensual dream of the night before after she'd fainted. There was another sign that she was beginning on a downward spiral of sexual perversion – what else would cause her to dream so vividly, orgasm so wildly?

She felt a small moistness at her crotch, and squeezed her thighs together, tightly, guiltily as though her excitement was visible.

Mrs. Simpson was the only one of the three of them who carried on a proper conversation during the meal; Jillian was too busy staring at Alison, teasing and caressing her genitals – and, before the meal was over, reaching an obscene climax and even shooting a little stream of clear juice that splattered onto the dining-room carpet, while she gave breathless, jerky groans. Alison herself was too engrossed with her own erotic fantasies to pay much heed to her employer's words.

She was glad when the meal was over and she could hurry up to her room, prepare herself, then run down to the waiting car and chauffeur.

* * *

"Doctor Bell's, please Sean," she said to the Irishman.

"Yes, Ma'am," he said, politely, adjusting his rear-view mirror so that he could see Alison's legs and thighs under her short skirt.

The car slid forward smoothly; Sean's eyes flicked to the mirror. She's not wearing stockings today! he exclaimed to himself. He stirred in the driver's seat. Alison's bare legs and thighs were visible up to her crotch. Cream silk briefs, smooth and clinging, and each time she moves her legs I can see strands of dark hair poking out from under her panties!

Sean's hand slipped onto his crotch and he felt the hard mass of engorged flesh there. I'll bet she's got a tight, snug pussy! Unobtrusively, he squeezed the swollen head of his cock. Unless that dykey little bitch, Jillian, has already got into her!

The car turned off the main highway onto a side road. Pretty face and figure – I'll bet her pussy's as soft as satin, as tight as a creamy glove!

"Is it far, Sean?" Alison asked.

He jerked his head, taking his hand from his crotch guiltily as Alison slid to the edge of her seat to speak to him.

"Just a few minutes, Miss," he answered, huskily.

Alison sat back and her skirt stayed dragged up. Bejasus! Her panties are so thin I can see her dark hairs through them! I always like a girl with a hairy cunt, always get a hard-on, a big stiffie, when the girl's young and hairy and wet! I'll bet she's wet and warm inside and as juicy a young morsel as I've ever seen!

He stopped the car outside a remote building that was more like a lodge than a house.

"We're there, Miss," he told Alison. "Doctor Bell's."

He slid out of the car quickly and opened the door for her. Glancing down at the bulge in Sean's trousers, Alison could see that the little show she'd put on for him in the back of the Bentley had had the desired effect and smiled a tight, secret little smile to herself as she sauntered up the short path to the front door of the lodge. Sean watched her buttocks work as she went, the light cotton skirt clinging sexily to the two perfect hemispheres as they jiggled and danced in a sexy contralateral motion.

Just the sight of her from the back excited him. I'll be screwing that sweet pussy of yours as soon as I get the chance, Miss Jeffreys, he promised himself and Alison beneath his breath. I'll be fucking that tight cunt before Jillian ruins it with her monstrous, beast-like dildoes! You'd better believe me, he fingered himself through the thick material of his uniform trousers, I'll be after squirting my juice in your hot, sweet pussy!

Alison had rung the bell; now the door was open and Sean watched her enter before he got back in the car to wait for her.

"I'm glad you could come," said Maurice Bell, leading Alison into a small room at the back of the lodge.

Alison looked around at the informal furnishings curiously; this wasn't like the doctors' offices she was used to in the city.

"Is this where you see your patients?" she asked.

Maurice hesitated, then said, "As a matter of fact, Alison, I'm not practising now – I'm sort of retired – I just see patients as a favour to friends."

"Like Mrs. Simpson," said Alison.

He gave her a sharp glance, but her expression was guileless.

"Yes," he said, his voice dry, "like Hermione Simpson."

He stopped at a high, cushion-covered bench that was more like a masseur's table than the conventional examining couch in most doctors' offices.

"How did you sleep last night?" he asked quietly.

Alison leaned against the bench. "Fine," she smiled into his face. "I didn't need to take the pill."

He smiled back at her. "Did you need anything else?"

Alison flushed then dropped her eyes, remembering his words about making herself come if she wanted to.

"I don't know what you mean," she mumbled.

"Yes, you do," he persisted. "Did you play with yourself before you went to sleep – did you tickle your clitoris and orgasm after I left you last night?"

The colour in her cheeks deepened. "Yes," she whispered, "I – I had to – I wanted to so much after – after the – the dream I'd had!"

"That's all right, Alison," he said, his

voice warm and understanding.

"You don't need to be shy with me. It's quite natural and normal – especially for a very highly sexed girl like you."

She lifted her eyes. "Highly sexed?"

He nodded. "Very."

"Am I really highly sexed? How do you know that?"

He smiled. "You're shy as well, but I'd believe that you have very erotic thoughts and feelings – isn't that true?"

She flushed again then frowned. "I don't know, Doctor, really I don't know."

"But you feel very passionate sometimes, don't you, Alison? You feel that you want some form of sexual outlet?"

"S... sometimes," she admitted.

"That's why I'm going to examine you – find out your sexual threshold."

"W-what!" Her face was shocked, eyes frightened. "Why?"

"I'm doing research. I'm very interested in the extent and intensity of orgasms."

Alison's mouth dropped open, then she gave a nervous laugh. "Interested in orgasms?" She laughed again. "I suppose you are at that!"

"Scientifically," he said.

"Of course." Her voice was dry.

"Clinical orgasms," he added.

"Yes," she said, "I suppose."

He pointed to the bench. "Will you lie on your back on this couch?"

Alison's face paled and she looked frightened.

Maurice took a step closer and wrapped his arm around her shoulders.

"Nothing to be frightened about, Alison. I won't hurt you and you'll find it a very pleasant examination – very satisfying, I know."

His words sent a little thrill through her body. Just what will he do? Is he going to make me orgasm? A sensuous ball of expectancy formed in the pit of her stomach.

"D'you want me to undress?" she whispered.

He looked at her very seriously. "Are you wearing panties?"

She nodded then said, "Of course."

"Then take them off – and, if you're wearing one, your brassiere."

Alison smiled. "I'm not wearing one today." She kicked off her shoes then reached under her skirt, slipped her fingers in the elastic waistband of her briefs and slid them off.

Slowly, seriously, she handed the tiny briefs to Maurice. He dropped them on a chair, nodded toward the couch and Alison climbed onto it.

She sat on the edge for a moment, looking at his face. "Are you – " she paused, swallowed, then said, "Are you going to climb on top of me?"

He stared at the sheen of dampness on her legs: she was sweating and excited.

"No," he told her, "I'm not going to climb on top of you; there are other ways – very enjoyable ways – of bringing you to an orgasm."

She flushed again then leaned back, flattened herself on the couch and closed her eyes.

Maurice stared at the young figure of the girl for a moment, holding his breath, admiring the sizeable, pink-nippled, up-thrust breasts, slim waist and deliciously shaped legs which stretched down from the hem of the skimpy skirt, then he reached to the front of her blouse, unbuttoned it and exposed the white, throbbing breasts.

Alison's eyes opened and her colour deepened. "D'you have to do that?"

He nodded, smiled reassuringly, then drew his fingertip across the nipple of a breast very gently. Alison stiffened, then the nipple protruded and hardened.

"Why'd you do that?" she asked in a whisper.

"Testing," he said softly.

She smiled, closed her eyes again.

He moved down the couch. "Now, open your legs," he urged gently. "And part your thighs!"

She kept her eyes closed but her legs and thighs parted widely. Maurice raised the short skirt to her waist, baring her thighs, belly and the dark triangle of hair at the base. He let his eyes rest on the brunette foliage for a moment, and then his gaze went down to the inverted tip of the triangle and the slight mound with its thin slit down the centre and the pouting vaginal lips on either side.

He reached down, placed a finger on either side of the slit then stretched it open. The lips curled open, showing pink, wet flesh within; at the top of the slit, the pea-sized clitoris was visible. He touched it... Alison drew in her breath with a hiss and tiny quivers ran across her belly.

"Lift up your knees," said Maurice softly, "and let them fall apart."

She did as he told her and he watched the vagina ooze open. Bending his head, he stared up into her vulva then moved his hand lower, opening the cheeks of her bottom and exposing the anal opening.

He touched the small, pinkish-brown star with his fingertip. Alison flinched, drew in her breath sharply, but said nothing.

"Did you ever have anything in there?" he asked her.

"No!" she shot out the word.

"A man never put his penis in your anus?" he persisted.

"No, no, no," she said, sounding almost angry. "I'd never let a chap stick his cock in me there!"

"But you yourself," he asked quietly, "didn't you ever touch that little hole with your finger – when you were playing with yourself – didn't you ever?"

She twisted her head to one side. "May – maybe just touch is all – "

"Just put your fingertip in very gently?"

"Yes," she whispered.

"And pull it in and out?"

"Maybe – just – just a little!"

"And you enjoyed it?" he asked.

"I – I – " she broke off.

"Did it increase the thrills," he went on, "while you were teasing your clitoris with one hand you pushed your finger in and out of your anus and it heightened the sensation?"

"Oh yes," she breathed, lifting her knees higher as she spoke, "it's pure heaven when I do that!"

"You get a thrill at your anus, too?"

"You mean in my bottom?"

"Yes," he said.

"Ohh," she sighed, "all inside my bum – it feels like it's on fire – the thrills run from my pussy to my clit, then shoot out of my bottom – it shatters right through me, I blast like mad!"

Maurice inserted his fingertip inside her anus, felt the wet, warm walls hugging it and was aware of the throbbing inside the arousing flesh.

"You'll enjoy this test," he promised her, withdrawing his finger completely then lightly touching her clitoris. "I'm going to run a very mild current – a mild electrical current – from your clitoris to your anus."

Alison tensed her body opened her mouth to voice a protest. Maurice leaned over her face, speaking softly, persuasively. "You're going to orgasm with more intensity than you ever imagined in your wildest, most erotic dreams, Alison. You're going on cloud nine and you'll love every sensual second of your trip!"

"You… it won't hurt me?" Her voice was frightened.

"Anything but!" he promised her.

He wheeled the small table beside the couch, and Alison lay still, her head turned, watching him. For goodness sake! That black box with things attached to it, Alison asked herself, what on earth would it do to my pussy?

There were two cables with small suction cups at the end; Maurice attached them to each of Alison's nipples. The cups fitted over her breasts, holding them with their own suction, and a spongy pad inside them pressed lightly on her nipples. The slight contact made her nipples get hard and Alison breathed hard with excitement, making her breasts rise and fall, but the movements did not dislodge the rubber cups.

Maurice took another cable from the box on top of the wheeled table; the cable had a slim, phallus-shaped silver electrode attached to the end of it. He dipped the end of it into a jar of white lubricating cream. He stretched the electric cord until it was between Alison's thighs, then, telling her to raise her knees and part them, he eased open her anus and slid the electrode inside.

"Does that hurt?" he asked solicitously.

"No... no, it doesn't," she murmured.

"I put a little cream on it before I inserted it," he told Alison. "Can you feel it inside you?"

She moved herself a little. "Yes," she told him, "but only just."

"Wriggle your bottom," he told her.

She squirmed herself, and then nodded. "Now I can feel it!"

"Good," he nodded. He moved beside the

table and put his hand on a black knob. "Tell me what you feel – if anything." He turned the knob very slightly.

Alison lay still for a moment, then her belly contracted and she half-lifted her buttocks.

"Now!" she said, breathlessly.

"What d'you feel?" he asked, eagerly.

"In – in my bum – it's sort-of warm – jerky and warm!" Her voice was excited and a thin rill of saliva drooled from the corner of her mouth.

"Does it hurt?" he asked quickly.

She shook her head. "Oh no! Not a bit! It's nice – all warm and nice!"

Maurice nodded and turned the mild current off.

"It's gone now," said Alison, a little sadly.

"You'll have it again, later," he promised, smiling at her and reaching to another control.

"Tell me what you feel."

Alison shook her head; she wriggled her breasts from side to side. "My – my nipples are getting hard," she whispered.

"Yes?" He turned the control again.

"They're hot – it's like little stabs running through my breasts and they're warm. The – the cups are sucking my breasts, pulling them out and I can feel the nipples – ooh, I'm getting excited – they're getting harder and harder!" She shook her breasts, licked her lips, opened and closed her eyes.

Maurice turned off the current.

"You'll have more of that later, Alison. Are you enjoying this test?"

She opened her eyes and smiled at him. "Yes, oh yes, but – " her lower lip trembled, "but I'm sort of afraid – what are you going to do next?"

"What d'you think?" he asked, stretching another cable from the black box.

"My... my pussy – you're going to do something to my pussy?"

There was another electrode attached to the end of this cable, too, held in place by a thick rubber strap which had suction cups at either end.

"Yes," said Maurice with a smile, "it's time for your... pussy!"

He clamped a suction cup on either hipbone so that the rubber strap stretched over the top of her vaginal slit. He adjusted the position of the electrode so that it was directly above her clitoris, and then tightened the strap so that the end of the electrode was pressing on the very apex of her clitoris.

"Feel that?" he asked.

"Yes," she whispered.

"What's it touching?"

"My – my pussy – "

"But what part of your pussy?"

"My... my thingy, you know... my... my clit!"

"Yes," he said, "your clitoris." He turned the dial of an indicator at the top of the box, watching Alison's face as he slowly increased the vibrations.

"Oooh, that's..." Alison squealed suddenly, bucking her pelvis, "... so good; it went right through me – right through my little thingy, my clit!"

"Hurt?" he asked.

Alison squirmed. "No, oh no – do it again, Doctor!"

"Later," he promised, turning the dial back to zero.

Alison turned her head, swivelling her eyes as Maurice picked up the slim rubber sheath.

"What's that?" she whispered.

He smiled. "Something to keep your pussy warm."

"You – you're going to put it in inside – push it into me?"

"Yes."

She looked puzzled. "It – it's rather small, isn't it, Doctor?"

He laughed. "You like big penises?"

She flushed, closed her eyes.

He leaned close, then murmured, "You like big cocks inside you?"

"Really, Doctor! The things you ask!" she protested, trying to sound shocked.

"Alison, tell me: d'you like big cocks up your pussy?"

"I... I haven't had that many – many cocks in me," she blurted out; then opening her eyes, and staring at Maurice, indignantly, "and none of them big, I mean, really big."

He held up the sheath, pressed a button at the end of it and the sheath seemed to inflate, becoming longer and thicker. "I can make this as thick as you like, Alison." His voice sounded excited for the first time. "I'm pushing it in your pussy then making it get bigger – you tell me when it's the size you like."

She blinked rapidly. "Is – is it hard? Will it hurt me?"

"It's pliable but hard enough. It won't hurt but it'll expand until it's pressing against all sides of your pussy, filling you completely, and it'll touch every sensitive spot inside you as I pull it and push it in and out."

"Oh, Doctor!"

Maurice once more opened the jar of lubricating cream and, taking a dollop onto his finger, smeared it on the sheath. "I'll make it soft and lubricated so that it'll slide in and out easily and smoothly; it'll adapt itself to the contours inside your vulva, pressing evenly all over, touching everything, thrilling you quite completely."

He held his breath, bent over her as she opened her thighs and lifted her buttocks with trembling eagerness, then inserted the end of the sheath between the shivering lips of her vagina.

"I'm pushing it in, Alison," he whispered, "and when it's all inside, I'll press the button and make it get bigger and bigger until you tell me to stop."

"Alright, Doctor, alright!" Alison's voice was high with excited anticipation.

The sheath slid through the curled open lips, piercing its path into the shivering flesh until its rounded end was flush with the top of Alison's vulva.

"It... it feels as if it's right at the back of my pussy – " she said, her voice quavering, "but you can... it can get thicker if... if you like!" She lifted her hips and slowly rotated her pelvis as Maurice touched the button and made the sheath expand.

Alison closed her eyes and held her breath as the thickness increased; every now and then she'd make a wet, sensuous sound as the expanding sheath titillated a fresh part of her sensitive vulva.

Maurice watched the slit stretch open; the soft labia lips flowered outward, showing wet, pink flesh until it seemed that the opening could not possibly get wider.

"Is that enough?" he asked, his finger ready to press the button and halt the expansion.

"Just – just a little bit more, Doctor. It's like – like nothing I ever imagined. I've never been so filled before!" Alison's voice was dreamy and breathless.

"All right," she said at last, and Maurice pressed the button, and then slid the sheath, not without a little resistance, out of her quivering, clinging vagina then pressed it upward again.

"Oh, like that, Doctor – oh, yes, like that!" Alison raised her pelvis, her belly tightening into stiff ridges of tension as the sheath penetrated her.

Maurice reached to the controls and switched on the power for the breast-pads.

Alison gave a low squeal of ecstasy when she felt the vibrations on her nipples.

"Feel it?" Maurice whispered.

"Oh yes, on my breasts – the tits are all hard!" She shook herself, making her breasts swing from side to side, but the pads stayed in place.

Maurice increased the power. Alison

squealed again, more loudly this time.

"It's super! Oh, Doctor – you're driving me wild. My nipples are on fire!" She twitched and jerked her whole body.

He manipulated the sheath, squeezing it in high, dragging it down slowly with sensual twistings.

"Inside my pussy – ooooh, all over it, every wet part!" She lifted her pelvis, undulated it and moaned. A dribble of saliva was trickling from her mouth and running down her chin until it dripped onto her neck.

Maurice reached for the control for the anal electrode and turned it on.

Alison's buttocks jerked, and Maurice, still holding the sheath in her vagina, let his hand move with her body.

"Inside my bum. Ooooh! It's all hot!" She bounced her buttocks up and down on the couch but the electrode was not dislodged.

He reached down and under her, pressing the electrode more deeply into her anus; her squeals became shriller.

"My bottom, Doctor – the cheeks are shaking like jelly – oooh, up my bum, right up the bottom hole. The jabs are shooting right into me!" Alison's voice was a soft torrent of sound.

Maurice reached for the control for the

electrode on her clitoris and gradually increased the power.

A new note came into Alison's voice; a pulse in her forehead started to twitch madly. The saliva that dripped from her mouth increased. She lifted her knees high, and then pulled them back into her belly. Maurice changed his grip on the sheath, reaching under her drawn-up legs, squeezing the length of the rubber tube to the top of her sexual sac.

"My clit!" Alison screamed. "It's out of control!"

Maurice glanced at it; the electrode was bobbing wildly on Alison's jerking clitoral head. Each time the electrode touched and sent a sharp stab of current into the little organ, Alison's face twitched, her knees pressed into her belly and the contraction of her muscles in her vaginal walls forced the sheath downward with intense pressure.

Each time the sheath was forced down, Maurice jammed it back up, and a fresh squeal of pleasure and pain would spew from Alison's lips.

She rolled herself upward and backward and Maurice saw her anus stretching open with the electrode projecting; he placed his finger on the end of it, pressing it in to the limit. Alison shrieked and her buttocks became a mass of quivering jelly.

He reached to the box and increased the power in the anal electrode. Her shrieks changed into a babbling stream of obscenity.

"It's shooting up my arse, I'm coming inside it! My bottom's on fire; that bloody fire in my arse is making me come. Ooh, Doctor – *I'm coming in my fucking arse*! It's fucking me inside my bottom and I'm creaming! *Oooooooh*!"

Maurice swung over the dial, and the current in the clitoral electrode went up to near its limit.

Alison's belly became a shivering mass of vibrating muscles and nerves.

He saw the clitoris quivering madly on the end of its stem, and then Alison reached down, pressed her fingers into the base of her belly and pushed upward with her pelvis. "*Fuck*," she screamed, pressing her clitoris against the electrode. "Fuck my clit, you little metal rod, fuck and fuck and fuck!" She writhed in a sexual frenzy. "*Doctor*!" she screamed, "Fuck my pussy with that rubber – make it get big and bigger, all inside me – all over my frigging pussy – I'm orgasming all over. Oh, Doctor – ooooh, I'm coming in every bloody part of me!"

Suddenly, Maurice released his grasp of the rubber sheath, leaving it thrust inside Alison's pussy, pressing against the utmost end, and stood beside the couch. His eyes were excited as he watched the squealing, writhing and orgasming girl – then he turned to the controls and switched them all full on.

Alison's gyrations became even more frenetic. Her arms waved in the air wildly, then she reached to her crotch and scratched at her clitoris, squeezing it, pressing it against the electrode with maniacal strength. Her bottom bounced up and down, and each time it squashed onto the couch, the electrode up her anus went in more deeply.

"*Ohhhh, Doctor*," she screamed. "Up my bloody arse, it's making me come. I'm coming all over, Doctor, I'm going mad!"

Maurice watched the trickle of seepage from her anus as she writhed in sexual agony. His breath came more quickly, then he reached to his own crotch and unfastened his trousers.

Alison's eyes rolled wildly; she was unaware of the man standing beside the couch, holding his enlarged cock in his hand.

Suddenly, Maurice reached to the black box and cut off the power in all the attachments. Alison continued to writhe, jerk and moan with frenzy.

He seized the dead electrode in her anus and yanked it out of the wet, squirming hole.

Her bottom still quivered, the cheeks opening and closing of their own accord.

He detached the electrode which had danced its dance of sexuality on her clitoris. The slender spire still jerked, writhed and bobbed. Maurice pulled the sheath from inside the palpitating pussy. Her vulva still quivered, the lips remaining agape even after the thick sheath was gone.

Maurice jerked the suction cups off her breasts; the nipples were red and iron-hard. He touched them – and Alison jerked frantically. "Squeeze them, Doctor – they're aching, *please* squeeze them!"

He took a nipple between a finger and thumb with either hand and squeezed with all his strength. Alison drooled; the unbearable pressure thrilled her. She jerked out her legs, straightened them, but her belly still throbbed; the lips of her vulva still opened and closed, sucked in, pushed out with wet, squashing regularity.

Each time she lifted her legs in the air, Maurice could see the anal hole squirming open, clenching shut, and he saw too the thick fluid that flowed out.

"Doctor," Alison gasped, her face white, "I'm still – *urgh* – orgasming, still coming. Make me stop, Doctor – it's really too much. I can't stand it any longer!" Her abdomen jerked up, then crunched down onto the couch.

Maurice licked his lips and held his penis gingerly between a finger and thumb. "I've turned the machine off, Alison – it'll take a little while for the effects to wear off your body."

"How long," Alison panted, "how bloody long?"

Maurice watched her clitoris vibrate crazily; then he saw by Alison's expression that she was having a more voluptuous orgasm than ever; he reached down, inserted his finger in her vulva and felt the walls hug it, release it then hug it again with a sweet, sensuous strength.

"Not too long now," he said quietly; gripping his penis as though he was holding it back.

"I'm coming again, Doctor – I'm having another bloody orgasm!" Her voice was tortured. Her whole body jerked, then she seized her nipples with both hands, pulling and twisting them with frantic insistence.

"Watching you like this excites me," Maurice said slowly, his voice filled with restrained excitement. "I can see your pussy jerking and squeezing its walls together and I want to stick my cock in it... you don't mind if I do, Alison?"

"Turn, urgh – turn off the current, Doctor, please!"

"It's already turned off, Alison, like I told you. You'll keep orgasming for a little while longer. I can't stop it." Maurice watched her jerking body for another second, then added, "Your threshold is quite something, Alison. You orgasm most intensely!"

Alison's eyes dilated. "Don't I know it!" she gasped, starting to rock into another shattering orgasm. "What're you going do to stop me, Doctor. Ooohh, Doctor – I'm coming again and it's hurting my pussy now – what will you do?"

Maurice licked at his lips. "I'd like to lie on top of you, Alison, insert my cock in your pussy and let you jerk and writhe and twitch until I orgasm!"

"I'm going potty and you want to fuck my cunt?" Her voice went high.

Maurice pursed his lips. "All I'd have to do is lie on you, Alison, and that squirming pussy of yours would do the rest."

"Oh, Doctor!" Alison jerked herself up and down. "It's like fire running from the hole in my bottom to my pussy. I'm coming *again*, Doctor. I'm orgasming – I can't stop *coming*!"

Wildly, Alison rolled from side to side on the couch. Her legs threshed the air and her arms waved, then she parted her legs to the limit, placed her fingers over her still bobbing and weaving clitoris. "I – I can't stop!" she panted, saliva running from her mouth in a stream.

Slowly, deliberately, Maurice climbed onto the end of the couch and slid his way up to her body. Her legs were outstretched on either side of him and when he let his weight go down onto her he could feel the violent shocks still tearing through her flesh. He reached under himself, seized his penis and guided it between her thighs. Her pelvis was jerking so much that it was difficult to steer his organ into her vulva, but when she raised herself as another orgasm rocked through her, he stabbed inward quickly with his erect cock and penetrated the writhing, squirming lips of her pussy.

The soft vaginal walls vibrated violently against his stiff cock.

"Oh, Alison," he moaned, "you're really the most delicious young thing!"

"Urgh," she groaned, "you're in me, I can feel your cock – you're actually going to fuck me!"

Maurice lay very still. "You're fucking *me*, Alison!" He gave an excited laugh. "This is heaven, Alison – just lying on your delicious, electrically charged body and letting your throbbing, jerking cunt suck every drop of juice from my cock!"

He held the cheeks of his bottom tightly together, savouring the thrills that coursed through his flesh as the soft, strong walls of Alison's quivering pussy caressed, squeezed and hugged his cock.

"Alison!" he shouted suddenly, "I'm going to come – I'm going to come inside you!"

"I – I've come so many times that – urgh, Doctor – I… I… think that I'm going to come again. Oh, Doctor, God almighty, all your stuff inside me, you're coming inside me – I can feel the hot, burning stuff in my pussy! Doctor, oooh!"

The groan throbbed from Maurice's throat as the sperm was sucked from the depths of his balls. The intense orgasm drained him of strength. Alison was still vibrating, still experiencing a waning series of lesser and lesser orgasms as he dragged his drained body off hers.

Weakly, he stood beside the couch watching her face, twisted and contorted with passion, excitement and fatigue as she shook, jerked, became orgasmic and then started the sensuous chain again.

Maurice glanced at his watch then sank onto a chair beside the couch to wait until the tortuous sequence of electrically induced orgasms came to an end.

* * *

Alison was weak and trembling when her vaginal spasms finally abated.

"Oh, Doctor," she moaned weakly, "that was really too much, I feel half-dead."

He got to his feet. "I'll get you a drink," he said. "You need one."

"Oh, my God – yes."

He poured her a stiff brandy and she drank it straight down, gagged, then blurted, "Why did you have to do that?"

Maurice had fastened his trousers and adjusted his clothing after his torrid sexual experience on top of the quivering girl and now he looked at her with raised eyebrows. "Didn't you want a drink?"

She gave a sarcastic laugh. "Very funny. You know that I didn't mean that... Why did you have to fuck me?"

Maurice looked at the girl who had seemed so shy when she entered the lodge that afternoon. It was a phenomenon that he had noticed before: his electrically induced orgasms seemed to remove mental as well as physical inhibitions.

He forced a smile on his face. "How could

I resist you?" he murmured.

"You were lying there so sexually desirable, with your little pussy jerking like mad as you orgasmed again and again – how could I resist such a soft, sweet fuck – and, Alison, it was the best. The very, very best!"

Despite herself, Alison smiled. "That doesn't sound very professional, Doctor."

"I didn't mean it to sound professional – you were quite irresistible, Alison." He gave her another smile, then sounded professional when he asked, "And how do you feel now?"

She sighed. "Drained... all drained out. I – I never came so much in my life."

"But do you feel satisfied?" he asked.

She nodded, then gave a shaky laugh. "I ought to feel bloody satisfied! If I don't feel satisfied after all those orgasms then I never will be!" She shook her head in wonder. "I've never been flying so high in all my life." She wriggled herself. "My bottom's sore – I even came inside my arse, I think – and my pussy's still throbbing and twitching whenever I move." She fondled her still-naked breasts. "My nipples are still on fire. I've only got to touch them to feel the start of a thrill."

"It'll wear off," said Maurice.

Alison was recovering fast. "I don't know whether I want it to wear off completely," she said, smiling. "It's pretty nice to feel thrilly and sexy like I do right now!"

Maurice smiled then glanced at his watch. "It's four o'clock. Your chauffeur is waiting outside."

Alison's expression changed. "Sean! I'd forgotten all about him. Gosh, Doctor B., I'd better get going."

She picked up her briefs, struggled into them, then buttoned her blouse.

Maurice escorted her to the door. "I hope you'll come again," he murmured before he let her out.

She nodded, then gave a giggle. "Don't you think I've come enough already, Doctor?"

He smiled after her as she wiggled down the pathway to the waiting car and Sean, who jumped from behind the wheel and opened the car door with alacrity.

She reacted, Maurice decided, closing the door and returning to his study, more voluptuously than anyone I have ever tested! I would certainly like to test her again. His penis moved, rubbing against his clothing as he mentally added: And fuck again, of course!

Alison pressed herself against the back of the seat. What an experience!

Sean glanced at her face in the car mirror as he started the engine.

"Are you all right, Miss?" he asked, then added, boldly, "What was it the doctor wanted?"

Alison could feel the lips of her vulva pressing against each other each time she took a deep breath.

"Just – just tests," she mumbled.

"Oh," said Sean. He had heard about Maurice Bell's tests. He could imagine some of the erotic things the ex-doctor had been doing. His penis reacted at his thoughts, then he wondered again when he would have the opportunity to sample Alison's fresh, young cunt.

Alison wriggled uncomfortably. The vibrations, which had pulsed through her pussy for so long, were having an unexpected effect upon her. She felt an urgent need to urinate. Moreover she had a wicked plan – which involved the virile body of Sean O'Toole.

"Sean," she shouted when the sensation became unbearable, "stop the car right now!"

The chauffeur brought the car to a jerky halt. They were still on the small side road, a considerable distance from the main road.

"What is it, Miss?" he asked, anxiously. "Are you feeling sick?"

Alison flushed with genuine

embarrassment. "No... I... I have to... you know... to do something, Sean, I can't wait..." She struggled with the door handle.

Understanding flooded Sean's face. He whipped open the door, glanced around him then nodded toward a clump of bushes.

"Over there, Miss – it's far enough from the road!"

Her flush deepened but Alison gave him a grateful smile as she hurried to where he had indicated.

Sean waited ten seconds then the stocky Irish chauffeur hurried after her.

He positioned himself very carefully, cunningly hidden.

Alison had her back to him and he could see everything clearly through an opening in the bushes. She lifted the back of her skirt, lowered the white panties that he had admired during the outward drive, then she crouched and he watched, enthralled, as a powerful stream of liquid gushed down from the hairy split of her vulva for what seemed like an eternity.

He could see her naked ivory buttocks and between them her tight little nut-brown anus, then below it, the sweet pink cleft, fringed by dark, curly hairs – he saw it all and it excited him beyond belief.

So close! So bloody close!

He clutched at the front of his trousers then ran round to the front of the bushes and confronted a startled Alison as she was about to drag up her panties.

She stood quite still, as if in shock, skirt lifted, exposing her pubic hair, fingers holding the waistband of her panties below her knees.

"Miss... Miss Jeffreys," he stammered. "I... I couldn't help seeing you and... and I... I..." He groped at the zip of his trousers, yanked it down, and his cock burst out. His breathing was loud and laboured. "I so want to fuck you, Miss Jeffreys, I... I can't help myself, I really must fuck your wet pussy!"

"W... why Sean, I... I... really, I don't know what to say!" Indeed, Alison was off-balance, utterly entranced by the sight of the Irishman's enormous, burgeoning cock; indeed, she began to wonder if she hadn't bitten off rather more than she could chew. She almost smiled at the unintentional pun. She stood as if petrified while the thickset man holding his big, stiff penis in his hand staggered towards her.

"I have to, Miss Jeffreys," he gasped. "I'm so sorry but I just have to!"

He reached to her body with his free hand, groping at her crotch until he found her still-wet vaginal lips.

"You're all wet," he said, his voice full of almost innocent wonder. "I knew you would be... I just knew it!"

She could feel his hot breath on her face as he pressed against her; then she lost her balance, falling backward, feeling his fingers prodding at her pussy, feeling it, squeezing it and rekindling her barely-subsided excitement and desire.

He dropped on top of her, his hard penis jammed against her belly and she realised with a perverse little thrill that no matter what she did he would fuck her; but she really didn't care, indeed, she relished the prospect: the residue of Dr. Bell's electrical stimulation was still flickering through her flesh.

"Please understand that I just can't control myself, Miss Jeffreys," he groaned, reaching underneath his body, seizing his swollen cock and steering it between her thighs.

Alison said nothing, but she allowed her legs to part as he squeezed himself between them.

Her pussy was still vibrating gently, and when the head of his organ penetrated her vaginal lips, she gave an involuntary gasp. He was big!

"I – I don't want to hurt you, Miss," Sean

muttered; it felt to him as if Alison's pussy were clutching at his cock, squeezing it and sucking it up inside her soft, warm cavern of delight. "I... I *have* to do what I'm doing... I just can't help it!" he groaned in an attempt to justify his abusive behaviour for the umpteenth time.

He drove himself inward, pulled out with sweet, sucking undulations and Alison let her sensitive, charged-up sexual organ respond. She thought: I'm going to orgasm again!

The shocking but thrilling thought zoomed through her mind as she felt her vagina hugging his jerking cock. She lifted her pelvis, pressing her excited clitoris against his solid shaft as the chauffeur neared his climax.

"Oh God, Miss Jeffreys, I can feel it happening!" he wailed, rocking himself madly, driving his cock hard in and out, "I'm going to shoot my spunk inside your sweet quim!" he gasped. "I'm coming! *Ugh*, Miss Jeffreys, now, *now*!"

His thickset body vibrated; shocks shattered through his flesh and Alison felt the powerful, thick squirts of warm white spunk spurting inside her pussy as a fresh orgasm racked her thoroughly aroused body. She started to climax, noisily.

"Ooohh," she moaned, "ooohh!"

The pure animal lust in Sean's mind waned. "I... I'm sorry, Miss," he mumbled, thinking Alison was moaning with pain. "I... I couldn't help myself!" He rolled off her limp body, and Alison turned her head then twisted herself onto her face in an effort to hide her very obvious lack of distress. But this coy manoeuvre had an entirely unexpected outcome.

He stared down at the naked bottom. It seemed to look back up at him, cheeky, inviting and yet – utterly vulnerable. He moved his hand to stroke it then stopped himself.

"You... you're such a sweet thing," he half-sobbed, remorse now flooding over him in a wave, "such a juicy young morsel, Miss Jeffreys – I couldn't resist you!"

He moved his hand again, and this time he allowed himself to stroke the luscious, prone bottom.

"I – I hate myself, Miss Jeffreys," he sobbed. "I shouldn't have done what I did. I hate myself!" His hand stroked the satiny flesh; then he drew his fingertip up the delicate cleft.

The anal opening was wet and warm. He felt it with his finger and as he touched it, his excitement was aroused anew.

"Soft, beautiful little arse," he

murmured, stroking the flesh, touching the small brown star. "Nice little hole, so moist and warm." He thrust his fingertip into the yielding sphincter and felt the anal walls cling to his finger. His penis reared again.

He grabbed at his organ as though he was trying to prevent it from performing without his permission, as it appeared to twist and lurch inside his grasp with a life all of its own.

"Ooooh, Miss Jeffreys," he moaned, "it's the lust for you… I have a terrible urge to… Well, I just have to bugger you!"

His whole body trembled but he rolled himself on top of the young girl's body and let his iron-hard cock-head come to rest at the pinkish-brown anal opening.

Fresh shock pulsed through Alison's body when she felt the weight of his body on her back. Again! He is going to fuck me again! Fuck me in my bottom hole! Bugger me! Really – this was too much – he's very big and it will probably hurt! She squirmed frantically, but there was no point – he was too heavy and strong. While she felt that she could have controlled the situation when he was fucking her face to face, in this position she felt completely powerless.

The end of his penis probed at the small, rosebud-like opening. Gradually, Alison's anal sphincter opened up as Sean pushed gently in. The electrode that had been inserted so sensuously and caused such voluptuous spasms had left a residue of erotic sensation within the soft, hugging anal canal.

Sean drove in with all his strength. He had expected that the young, unused flesh would resist his enlarged organ, but the palpitating, still-aroused flesh received his cock with a smooth, almost sucking motion. He penetrated deeply, and Alison gave yet another low moan.

She could feel her anal walls sucking and hugging the snake-like, twisting intruder. It was the first time she'd had a cock inside her anus, but the sensation was far from unpleasant. Instead of rending and tearing her as she had worried it might do, the shaft slid in easily, far into the depths of her rectum, titillating sensitive walls and sending delicious thrills rippling from her bottom to her pussy and tingling around her clitoris.

Sean let the air spurt out of his lungs. This sweet, young arse was sucking his cock with sensuous delight. He'd never thrilled so intensely to any sexual experience.

Once again, his large, heavy balls tightened inside the fleshy sac; he felt the sperm streaming to the base of his cock, jerking down its length then spurting from its oh-so-sensitive tip.

"Ohhh!" he groaned as the scalding juice squirted into Alison's virginal anus. "Your luscious little arse! Oh, Miss Jeffreys – I've fucked your snug, tight little arse!"

He rolled off the young, used and abused body, and dragged great gulps of air into his lungs; then once more, belated remorse flooded his being.

"I – I couldn't help it, Miss Jeffreys – I couldn't help it!" he sobbed.

Alison turned herself very slowly. When this carnal man had spurted inside her bottom, she had experienced a searing, thrilling orgasm like she'd never had before. But, of course, Sean didn't need to know that!

She made her voice sound angry and bitter. *"You raped me!"*

Sean's face twisted. "M... Miss Jeffreys – I... I couldn't help it. You're so tempting, so delicious, I... I..." he broke off, restraining his sobs only with effort.

Alison herself sounded as though she was going to cry. "You – you fucked me in my pussy squirting all your horrible stuff, and then – " she broke off, as if to choke back her tears. "You did it up my bottom, buggering me, hurting me – why did you... *how* could you... do this to me?"

Sean lifted a hand to stroke her then

stopped himself. "Please, Miss Jeffreys, I'm so sorry. Really I am. It – it's because you're so desirable, so lovely – I couldn't help it. You're the most desirable woman I've ever seen!"

Underneath her stern facade, Alison felt an uncontrollable surge of pleasure at the blurted words. Hmm... am I really so irresistible? She stopped herself from smiling with an effort, and managed to make her voice severe when she said, "What'll happen to you when I tell Mrs. Simpson what you've done to me?"

He dropped his eyes, shuddered then muttered, "Oh, Miss Jeffreys – she'll whip me, then sack me. I'll be finished!" His face was white with fear and remorse.

"You realise that after what you've done," said Alison very slowly, "you leave me no choice but to tell her."

Sean shivered. "Miss, you – you can do anything you like to me – anything at all, but please don't report this to Mrs. Simpson!"

"But what else is there for me to do?"

A glimmer of hope came into Sean's eyes. "You – you can punish me yourself, Miss Jeffreys. You can do anything you like to me to make it right. I'll let you do anything to me: I'll do anything you say – anything, Miss Jeffreys!"

She made her voice puzzled. "Punish you?"

He nodded eagerly. "Like Mrs. Simpson does. She punishes the staff instead of firing them."

Mrs. Simpson's words in the office came back into Alison's mind: discipline!

"How does Mrs. Simpson punish you?" she asked.

Sean answered very quietly. "Beats me with her hand or a strap or a whip."

"Beats you?"

He nodded, dropping his eyes. "Other things, too." He swallowed, "She makes me do things for her... to her..."

"Like what?"

His voice dropped to a whisper. "She makes me kiss her and suck her pussy until she comes!"

An insane thrill surged through Alison's belly.

"And then she'll beat me," Sean went on. "Stick the butt-end of her whip in me then make me suck her... " his voice went even lower, "...in all places, in all kinds of ways!"

Alison was silent, keeping her eyes shielded to hide the gleam of excitement.

"You can do what you like to me, Miss, as long as you don't tell Mrs. Simpson."

Alison licked her lips.

"You can beat me until I bleed... "

"I wouldn't want to do that," Alison whispered.

"I'll do anything you like to you – I'll suck your pussy all night if – if you'd like it! I'll suck you anywhere, do anything, Miss Jeffreys – anything!"

Alison got to her feet and pulled up her underwear. Involuntary little spurts of Sean O'Toole's semen dribbled from both of her thoroughly gratified orifices and she could feel the gusset of her panties become soaking wet with the residue of his ejaculate. She glared down at Sean and he got to his feet like a dog that was about to be whipped.

"I won't talk to Mrs. Simpson – not immediately, anyway," said Alison, coldly.

Sean gave her a pathetically grateful smile.

"Now help me back to the car," Alison snapped. He sprang to her side, took her arm and helped her over the rough terrain then whipped open the car door and helped her inside.

"Later, I'll decide how to punish you..." said Alison when Sean was back in the driver's seat, "decide what I want to do to you – or have you do to me, if anything."

"Thank you, Miss Jeffreys," Sean said hoarsely. "I'm very sorry for what I did, and

I'm grateful to you."

"I won't forget what you said – or did," Alison said severely. "From now on you'll do anything and everything I tell you!"

"Oh yes, Miss Jeffreys. Anything – any time!"

"Very well!" said Alison with a new voice of authority, sinking back into the luxury of the Bentley's leather seats. "Now, drive me back to Lazonby!"

"Yes, Miss," Sean said submissively, driving toward the main road.

Chapter 7

"Are you all right?"

The cool question made Alison pause as she was hurrying through the front hall at Lazonby on her way to her room to freshen up and compose herself after Sean had dropped her off at the front door.

"W… why yes, Mrs. Simpson," Alison stammered.

The mistress of Lazonby Hall surveyed Alison's flushed face, over-bright eyes and keyed-up manner.

"What did – " she paused, "the doctor want to see you about?"

"Oh," Alison's flush deepened, "just... just some tests." She dropped her eyes as she spoke.

"I see," Hermione said very softly. She took a deep breath, then said, "Well, you'd better get along upstairs and prepare yourself for dinner. Jillian and I will be waiting." She turned and entered the dining room as Alison hurried up the stairs.

* * *

Jillian was standing at the old-fashioned bay window, looking out into the garden. She didn't turn, recognising her mother's footsteps, and simply asked, "Is she back?"

"Yes," said Hermione, crossing the room and standing beside her daughter, who was rather unusually wearing a short tartan skirt.

She made a small sound and Hermione glanced at her face. Her mouth was a little open, the tip of her pink tongue protruding. "My little Alison," she sighed beneath her breath, "my own little Alison, all mine, to play with as I like!" Jillian's tongue caressed the underside of her upper lip in a visible display of sensual yearning.

"Yes," said Hermione, slowly, "I suppose she is." Her eyes went down and she added, "Just now, it would seem that you're playing with something else. Oh, Jillian, do you always have to be masturbating in public?"

She stared at the large, pink rubber dildo that she could see Jillian's hand grasping under the short hiked-up skirt.

"I wish you wouldn't do that in here, dear," she murmured, her eyes still on the pink shaft that appeared and disappeared as Jillian thrust it upwards into her body. "Someone might walk in." She turned her head, jerked her eyes towards the door, then glanced down again. "You're so wet," she whispered, "always so wet!" Her hand moved down and she felt her daughter's sopping sex with her fingers.

Jillian made a sound like a sob, took her hand off her dildo and gave her mother a grateful look. "Please do it for me, Mummy! It's so nice when you do!"

Hermione squeezed the rubbery shaft, and felt it quiver slightly under her fingers as Jillian's cunt started to convulse with little spasms, then sighed. "How many times have you done this today?"

Her daughter arched her back with pleasure as she bucked under Hermione's gentle caresses. "You mean, brought myself off?"

"Yes," she murmured, standing very close, now thrusting the obscene phallus more deeply into Jillian. "How many times today?"

"Just... just two times, Mummy," she panted, throwing her head back and opening her mouth wider as the fingers of her mother's other hand joined to skilfully manipulate her clitoris. "This... this morning," she gasped, "when I... I watched her getting out of bed, getting dressed..."

"You were in the spare room, watching through the transom?"

"Yesss, Mummy, oh yes! She has such a beautiful body, Mummy. It's all soft, creamy and delicious, and she has the most beautiful tits and pussy."

"I've no doubt that she does," murmured Hermione, colouring slightly and sliding her hand further under Jillian's until she could feel the little pucker of the girl's anus. She introduced the tip of her slippery finger.

"That's so nice, Mummy; I love it when you play with my bottom-hole."

"You masturbated when you were watching Alison getting dressed?"

"Yes, Mummy," she groaned, feeling the knowing fingers slide onto her clitoris again. "Oh, yes – and again – at lunch."

Hermione made a sound that could have been resignation or exasperation.

"I thought you were doing that at lunch

time!" she sighed, and continued to stroke her daughter's inflamed labia with one hand while she thrust the pink rubber dildo in and out of her with the other.

Jillian made a funny little sound that her mother recognised as the prelude to an orgasm. She whisked the dildo out just in time to see a jet of clear liquid splash against the window.

"Oh, Jillian dear, please don't spurt all over the dining-room carpet – I've just had it cleaned!"

Her daughter gave a breathless, deep-throated chuckle as she tilted her pelvis forward once more and again the passion gripped her body.

"Again, Mummy! Sorry – ohhh… shit… fuck! Shit! I'm coming again!" She reared her head back, opened her mouth and gulped in air as she shot another stream of thick juice onto the window-pane that dribbled down to the floor. Some trickled over Hermione's hand, still busy ministering to her daughter's sex.

Hermione's body tensed with excitement: she pressed herself forward and gripped the obscene pink phallus in her clenched fist; she waited until Jillian gave her last shudder and then stepped back, removing a dainty handkerchief from her sleeve.

"You've done it again, Jillian," she said, resignedly, wiping the stickiness off her hand. "I'll have to go and wash before dinner. And I've told you about using bad language. I don't like it!"

"That was lovely, Mummy. And what's more it's reminded me of something I meant to tell you about Alison." Jillian leant forward conspiratorially. "You'll never guess, but she's a squirter, too!" Then she gave her mother a contented smile, "Oh thank you, Mummy! You always make me come so nicely."

A faint smile also lightened Hermione's expression. "I'm glad you enjoyed it, dear."

She moved toward the door, but Jillian called after her: "Mummy! Tonight – do you think I'll be able to play with Alison tonight?"

Hermione hesitated, and a thoughtful frown creased her brow. She pursed her lips. "Well, maybe, dear…"

"Is Doctor Maurice coming for dinner, Mummy? Then can he stick his needle in her, you know, make her sleepy so I can fuck her?"

"No, Doctor Maurice's not coming tonight, dear, but – " she pursed her lips again, "perhaps you won't need any help – she's been having some tests, and," her voice dropped down as though she was talking to herself rather than Jillian, "she'll be feeling very passionate – I know what those tests do to your vulva and clitoris, getting them all worked up and hot and probably wanting some sexual release..." Her voice faded off, then she jerked her head and stared at her daughter. "I'll talk to you after dinner, Jillian dear, but in the meantime... behave!" The smile she gave her handsome, fresh-faced daughter took the sting out of the words.

* * *

Naked, Alison walked from her private bathroom into her bedroom. Her hands moved continually, stroking her breasts, caressing each stiff nipple in turn, then her belly and the flesh on her inner thighs. Each time her fingers strayed toward the pink, warm lips that flared open so suggestively beneath the wet thatch of pubic hair, but she restrained them with an effort.

Damn that doctor and his tests! Alison walked to her wardrobe and selected a dress. Each time she moved she felt her vaginal lips undulating, and her clitoris felt like a wriggling, hungry worm. I feel so bloody randy! I'd like to lie on my back on my bed and squeeze my clit til I come!

Her breasts were so up-thrust that a

brassiere was really superfluous, so Alison dragged the dress over her head. She reached for a fresh pair of panties to replace the ones that Sean, in the heat of his violent passions, had ripped, then changed her mind.

Alison stood still for a minute, thinking; and as she thought, her hand slipped under the front of her short dress and she caressed the waiting, hungry lips with a fingertip.

Jillian with her carnal, lesbian hungers! No doubt she'll be grovelling under the table at dinnertime, staring under my skirt then playing with herself... This time, perhaps I'll give her something to see that she won't forget. I'll drag my skirt high, hold my knees apart and let her feast her lecherous young eyes on my pantiless pussy!

Alison giggled aloud at her thoughts. She'll probably shoot straight through the tabletop! And what would dear Mrs. Simpson do then?

Suddenly, she stopped giggling. Jillian might take it as an invitation, and get so worked up that she'd come to my room and try to rape me! She felt her clitoris twitch at the thought. What would it feel like to be in bed with another girl? She had only had asexual experiences at her boarding school – nothing sexual at all, really. This would be different. What would Jillian want to do to me? Stick her fingers into my pussy? Rub her pussy against mine? Make me kiss her pussy? Oh no! It would be awful! Surely I wouldn't want that... would I ? Oh my God, why am I so wet now? Am I a raving lesbian, too?

Alison let out her breath, pulling her hand from under her skirt with an effort. Anyway, Mrs. Simpson wouldn't let anything like that happen to me!

She combed her hair carefully, took a towel and dabbed, daintily, between her thighs until most of the moistness was gone, then, after arranging her face into an expression of suitable modesty, Alison went demurely downstairs to dinner.

* * *

"The Somerset air seems to be doing you good, Alison," said Hermione drily during dinner. "You look positively radiant this evening!"

Alison flushed, and gave her employer a quick glance to see if she was being sarcastic, but Mrs. Simpson looked innocent and sincere.

"Thank you," she said, smiling. "I'm afraid I haven't done much work yet to justify that generous salary you're paying me."

"Don't worry about that, Alison dear," said Hermione. She gave a light laugh and added, "Oh, you'll earn it, my girl!"

Jillian giggled, as if she was sharing a private joke with her mother. So far, Alison had noticed, she has not stooped under the table once! No sooner had the thought left her mind than Jillian dropped her napkin, bent low to get it and her head disappeared under the table.

Feeling wicked, Alison dragged her skirt up to her crotch, parted her knees then, casually, let her hand fall onto her lap and glide lower and lower until her fingers were touching her wet vaginal lips. Slowly, she spread them open with her fingers.

Sounds of slight movement came from underneath the table while Hermione and Alison chatted desultorily.

Finally, Hermione snapped, "Jillian! What on earth are you doing under there?" And Alison saw her move as though she was giving her daughter a hefty kick.

Slowly, Jillian's face came into view; her face was very pink and covered in a light sheen of sweat. Her lips quivered as if she had just experienced some deep emotion and she took deep, painful gulps of air.

"My... my napkin, Mummy," she gasped. "I... I just dropped it, that's all."

And Jillian smiled as if disappearing under the dinner table for minutes at a time was the most normal thing in the world.

Alison saw Jillian's hand go under the table and her body started squirming.

Hermione gave her a sharp glance. "Jillian," she muttered sharply, half-closing her eyes, "Jillian, please!" Suddenly, Hermione started talking to Alison with great animation about the latest news, the weather, the Somerset countryside... until Alison realised that she was trying to distract her attention from Jillian, who was obviously, and with great, panting enjoyment, masturbating hard under the dinner table.

* * *

Sean rubbed himself against Rosie when she came back into the kitchen after serving coffee in the dining-room. "I feel like it," he mumbled.

"I want you to suck me off!"

Rosie whirled, her face angry. "I saw you – when you were serving her dessert!"

He drew back. "What?"

"That girl, Alison Jeffreys, you were staring at her legs – and more!" Rosie took a jerky breath. "I could see that the little bitch had her skirt pulled up to her belly, an' you leaning over her, starin' at her thighs an' the bit o' hair she got in between!"

"You're crazy!" Sean snapped, but he tried to loosen his trousers at the crotch as he spoke.

"It's her got you worked up – that's why you've got a stiffie. You an' your damned cock!" Rosie sneered viciously.

Sean coloured with anger; he took a step closer then reached up to her head, grabbed her hair and pulled until she went down onto her knees, moaning.

"Then suck it!" he ordered, ripping open his trousers with his free hand, pulling out his cock and thrusting it into Rosie's face.

Rosie moaned with pain as he cruelly twisted her corn-blonde hair, then babbled, "All right, Sean – stop pulling, you're tearin' my hair out by the roots – stop pullin', I'll suck your blasted cock!"

Her face moved forward, mouth open, and her lips seized the red, swollen ball at the end of his shaft.

"Urgh, that's better, urgh!" Sean rocked himself very slowly as Rosie's head bobbed back and forward. "Oh, suck it – keep sucking!" He squeezed the cheeks of his bottom together, pressed his pelvis forward and took loud, rasping breaths.

They were so engrossed that neither of

them knew that anyone had entered the kitchen until Hermione spoke.

"This seems to be a daily habit!" Her voice was cold and angry.

Rosie's lips plopped off Sean's cock, and the organ stuck out stiffly as Sean froze, then it jerked and spurted, Hermione watching as the white blobs squirted out then dropped onto the kitchen floor.

"All over the bloody floor," Hermione muttered, watching the pearly blobs as they landed. She narrowed her eyes, and sighed, "All over the bloody manor!"

Her lips tightened she spoke grimly, then: "Needless to say, I'll see you both in my room tonight before you go to bed. In the meantime," she added, sarcastically, "I came to ask for some more coffee – like everything else in this place, the bell doesn't work!" She turned and walked stiffly out of the kitchen.

White-faced, Sean stuffed his damp penis back in his trousers and fastened them. Rosie picked up the coffee-pot, trying to blink away her tears before she moved unsteadily into the dining room.

* * *

As soon as Hermione had left for the kitchen, Alison leaned down and looked under the table. Jillian's trousers were yawning open, and she could just make out the girl's pubic bush and her pink, engorged sex lips. She straightened herself and smiled at the awed young lesbian.

"It's hot, isn't it?" Alison said, brightly.

Jillian, mouth still open, nodded dumbly.

Alison rose to her feet and moved round the table until she was beside the teenager. Jillian's eyes followed Alison as though she were mesmerised by the older girl. "May I?" Alison asked, reaching for her napkin and taking it from beside her empty plate.

"Mmm!" was all Jillian could say. Her eyes watched what Alison was doing.

"When it's hot like this," said Alison, folding the napkin into a ball, "I always seem to sweat so much." She lifted the front of her short skirt, exposing her belly with the thatch of brunette hairs and wet, pink lips below; then, bending her knees slightly, she thrust her pelvis forwards and upwards so that her whole pudendum was well exposed, and with the napkin, wiped at the warm vaginal lips. She bent down so that her head was next to Jillian's. "What's more, my cunt gets all hot and wet," she whispered in Jillian's ear with a breathy giggle; then she dropped the used napkin in the girl's lap, returned to her place and was sitting, primly demure, in her place when Hermione returned to the room.

There was a dazed expression on Jillian's face as her lips moved and she struggled to speak. "Fucking hell…" she managed to gasp in a small voice. "Alison just… her wet cunt… I mean she…!"

"Jillian!" Hermione reprimanded. "Please don't say those vulgar words, dear." She turned to Alison with a strained smile. "Teenagers! The language they use these days! Alison, please don't pay any attention to the silly girl."

Alison just smiled, shyly.

Rosie approached the table with the coffee.

"And bring me my favourite liqueur," said Hermione.

"Yes, Ma'am," said Rosie. She returned with a tray, bearing three glasses and a decanter of crème de menthe.

Hermione poured the drinks herself, handing one glass to Jillian, another to Alison.

"That's all," she said to Rosie, then dropped her voice, "and don't forget to see me tonight."

"Very good, Madam," murmured the cook.

"Sean, too," said Hermione.

"I'll tell him, Ma'am," Rosie whispered, looking stricken. Alison sipped her drink, savouring the minty sweetness.

"They're such devoted servants," said Hermione, lifting her glass. "They do anything I tell them!" She drained her drink.

"I'm sure they do," said Alison, thinking of what Sean had said about his mistress that afternoon. She, too, finished her drink, and felt it warming her belly and flowing lower. She squirmed; the liquor seemed to reactivate the electricity in her body; she felt throbs in her abdomen, then in her pussy and all at once she felt that she wanted to urinate. That reminded her of Sean... The thing he did to me! I pressed my thighs together, his big cock squeezing into my pussy – then into the little hole in my bottom. It should have hurt – but it thrilled me instead... thrilled me so intensely! That thick, long cock!

Alison lifted her eyes, stared across the table and met Jillian's stare. She had gulped her drink down, and now her lips were apart and her eyes were fixed on her face. In the dim, candlelit room, she looked more androgynous than ever. She tried to say something but was sharply interrupted by her mother.

"Jillian!" Hermione said. "We'll talk

later." Her eyes blazed at her daughter who lapsed into a brooding silence. "Now, Alison," said Hermione with a change of tone, "won't you have another drink?"

"Well," Alison seemed to hesitate, "I'm really not very used to liqueur, Mrs. Simpson – if I have much more, I won't know what I'm doing!"

"Let us worry about that," said Hermione, refilling Alison's glass generously.

Jillian gave another seemingly motiveless laugh, picked up her napkin and smelled it – then began to suck it, loudly, with her firm, sensual lips.

Chapter 8

"She's a little strange," said Hermione, "but very affectionate and loving." She laughed, gently. "Sometimes she reminds me of a big, friendly dog that wants to paw you and lick you all over."

Alison half-choked over her drink. *She'll do more than paw me if she gets half a chance!*

They were sitting, Hermione and Alison, at the dining-room window, sipping their third glasses of liqueur and watching Jillian as she ambled about aimlessly in the grounds of the manor.

Hermione took out a cigarette and lit it without offering one to Alison.

"She's a very – " she drew in smoke then expelled it, "tomboyish girl," she said, carefully, "very mature and well-developed in some ways – immature and silly in others. It's hard on her sometimes, being cooped up here. She has no – no outlet for her – her energies; it makes her nervous at times, and excitable..." Her voice trailed off and she sipped at her drink, thoughtfully. When she spoke again, it was as if she was changing the subject. "How do you like being here, Alison, at Lazonby?"

The liqueur had made Alison feel relaxed and mellow; her body still felt sexually excited and thrills continued to ripple, at unexpected moments, from her belly to her clitoris, but she was getting used to her state of sexual arousal and the constant sensation of eroticism was becoming intensely enjoyable.

"I like it here, Mrs. Simpson," she told her employer, "but I haven't done much work for you yet."

"You will in time," said Hermione. She smiled at the young girl; noticed how she was holding her thighs pressed tightly together, and how tiny ripples ran across her flesh from time to time.

"You're a very pretty girl, Alison; very attractive."

Alison glanced at her employer, blushed sweetly, then said, "Thank you, Mrs. Simpson. It's kind of you to say that."

"It's perfectly true, Alison. You have a wonderful figure – a very enticing figure." She paused, adding, "You don't have to call me Mrs. Simpson – my name's Hermione."

Alison nodded, sipping at her drink again. The liqueur was going to her head.

"Have you quite a... passionate nature?" Hermione asked very softly.

"Well," Alison hesitated, "I... I don't know – perhaps I do."

"When I was your age I was very passionate," Hermione laughed, "still am, in fact." She kept her eyes on Alison's face until Alison met her gaze. "I still enjoy my diversions," she said quietly. "I have ways of appeasing my demands."

Alison glanced at Hermione's set expression, then emboldened by the drinks, she said, "By disciplining your staff?"

Hermione's mouth relaxed, then she laughed. "That's one of my foibles." She leaned forward, speaking eagerly, "I have some discipline to administer tonight – would you like to watch?"

The little thrill spiralled round Alison's navel then zoomed down. "H... How? How could I help?" Her voice was excited.

"I have to punish my cook and chauffeur for performing an unspeakable act in the kitchen this afternoon; if you'd like to be an observer, you can come to my bedroom tonight."

What would I do? The exciting question flickered in erotic circles from Alison's mind to her belly, making her tighten her abdominal muscles and squeeze her thighs together even more tightly. What weird act would this cold, haughty woman perform upon the helpless flesh of her servants?

"I – I think I'd like to," she whispered, "but – but wouldn't they mind my watching?"

"*Mind*?" Hermione echoed. "Sean and Rosie? It doesn't matter whether they mind or not – I'm the mistress of Lazonby!"

"Oh, yes – of course," murmured Alison.

Hermione turned her head, staring through the window. "Where's Jillian?"

Alison strained her eyes in the dusk. "She's at the far end of the grounds, standing beside a tree," she replied, peering through the gloom. "She seems to be moving herself back and forward, I don't know what she's doing."

"I can imagine," said Hermione, drily, getting to her feet and moving to the door. "Don't forget, Alison, be in my bedroom at about ten o'clock!"

"Y-yes, Mrs. – I mean, Hermione," said Alison, calling her employer by her first name for the first time. "I'll be there!" And she felt a crazy tingling of erotic anticipation at the base of her spine – and between her thighs.

*　*　*

Jillian was in her room. She had opened the top drawer of a chest of drawers and was studying the contents. Inside there lay a most extraordinary selection of dildoes, ranging from the small to the enormous, doubles, singles and strap-ons. Jillian reached down and selected the biggest.

*　*　*

Alison glanced at her watch; it was five minutes to ten. A fresh tremor of excitement flickered through her consciousness. It's time to go to Hermione's room and watch the performance! Alison giggled; she felt a little drunk with liqueur and anticipation. She passed her hand across her breasts, felt the nipples hard and stiff. I feel so worked up that I might even come – really come – just by watching Hermione spanking their naked bodies she thought!

"Come in, my dear, come in," Hermione said when Alison tapped at her bedroom door.

Alison stared in surprise at her employer. Hermione had changed her clothes; she was wearing her short leather skirt, high leather boots which came to above her knees and a skimpy leather halter.

She became aware of Alison's gaze, and laughed. "Do you like my outfit?"

She spun around for Alison's benefit.

The leather skirt lifted as she spun, and Alison saw that her employer was nude beneath the leather. Above the high boots, her bare legs gleamed and Alison was surprised at how well-shaped, how firmly fleshed, they were. Her naked buttocks were rounded and plump, and Alison thought she could detect very faint lines across the whiteness as though the mistress of Lazonby had, herself, been disciplined some time in the recent past. Who disciplines the disciplinarian? she wondered.

"Well?" Hermione asked when Alison didn't answer the question.

"Super!" enthused Alison. "It looks… well… very exciting!" she said.

Hermione smiled with pride. Her eyes were over-bright and there were two livid spots, high on her cheeks, which gave the appearance of her having a slight fever.

"I'm glad you think that," said Hermione. "That's how I want to look – that's how I feel." She moved up to Alison, wrapping her arm around her shoulders as she led her into the bedroom. "You look nice, Alison, but…" and she pulled her round to look into her face, then spoke intimately, "I have something to give you, something that I don't wear any more. I think it'll fit – and suit you – perfectly."

She rummaged in a drawer, then took out a flimsy piece of silk, holding it up in front of Alison's face.

"It's rather American – a shortie-nightie for a baby-doll!" She laughed very softly, and held it against Alison's body. "Put it on!"

Alison was startled. "Right away?"

Hermione nodded eagerly.

Shyly, Alison struggled out of her dress. Hermione drew in her breath when she saw that Alison was completely nude beneath. "Your figure, Alison darling, is completely delicious!" Her eyes roved hungrily over her young employee's firm flesh. "Turn around," she whispered.

Alison turned; Hermione focused her eyes on the rounded bottom.

"You've got the most delightful little bottom, Alison darling," Hermione laughed, breathlessly. "You make me want to dream up an excuse to spank that tempting flesh." She moved up to the young girl, let her hand drop on her buttocks, stroke gently then probe in the cleft. "You're adorable, Alison..." she whispered, touching the young girl's anal orifice with her fingertip, "... so very, very sweet!"

Alison's face was hot; she picked up the baby-doll nightie with fingers that trembled. "I... I suppose I'd better put this on," she mumbled.

"Oh, yes," whispered Hermione.

The nightie was so short that its hem was above the base of Alison's pubic triangle, and when she turned, the crevice of flesh that crossed in a delightful hollow below the rounded bottom was clearly visible.

"I'm so glad you're here!" Hermione said devoutly, pressing her hand between her own thighs and leaning forward as though she was holding something inside her crotch, "so very glad!"

The tips of Alison's pink nipples were visible through the transparent silk, and the rustle of the fabric made her think of static electricity. Electricity! All inside me – I've had electrodes in my pussy and up my bottom. No wonder I'm excited, worked up and passionate. I want to play with my clit and tickle my pussy – I'm so bloody excited I want to orgasm right now!

"You look very tense!" Hermione murmured. Alison nodded, then swallowed.

"You're ready to watch the discipline – is that what's exciting you?"

"Y... yes, partly – and... " Alison hesitated.

Hermione nodded in understanding. "This afternoon – the electrodes haven't worn off – "

Alison was startled. "You... you know?"

Hermione nodded again. "I know all about Maurice's 'tests'." She gave a short laugh. "We'll have to see what we can do –" She let her voice trail off.

"Shall we call in the..." she hesitated, then laughed and said: "... victims?"

Alison flushed, then nodded. Hermione went to her bedroom door, opened it and said, "You can come in now – both of you!"

Alison watched as Rosie and Sean ambled into the room. The chauffeur didn't look like the same aggressive man who had raped her – or rather, double-raped her – in the bushes that afternoon.

"Get the punishment stool, Rosie," Hermione snapped.

Rosie shivered with fear. "Oh, no, Ma'am – not that, please not that!"

Hermione picked up a short whip off her dresser top and showed it to the pretty, buxom, blonde cook. "Please don't make me angry, Rosie!" Her voice was taut with menace.

Rosie shivered again as she went to a closet and dragged out a bizarre piece of furniture. It was something in between the kind of vaulting horse that was used in gymnasiums and an old-fashioned praying pew. The top was covered with leather and it had four sturdy, sloping legs.

The cook dragged it into the centre of the bedroom, then stood, shaking, beside it.

"Now undress, both of you, completely!" Hermione snapped.

Alison's eyes flickered wildly from the disrobing figures to the weird contrivance on the floor. There were leather straps, with cuffs attached, fastened to each leg. What in the world are they for? Alison wondered. Her eyes skimmed back to the cook and the chauffeur.

Apart from startled glances when they had first entered the room, the two servants had ignored Alison's presence in their mistress' bedroom. Now, Alison observed the shivering, voluptuous flesh of Rosie's belly, bottom and thighs. Her breasts, too, were magnificent: big and full, they hung down low when she removed her brassiere, and the nipples were over-large with flattened tips as though they'd been pinched, bitten or abused too many times. The ample cheeks of her bottom spread open when she bent to remove her panties, and Alison stared at the gloriously smooth expanse of flesh, the wide cleft with a growth of hair between and the back of her sex, its rosy lips full and slightly agape with the pucker of her anus like a pale brown rosette perched above.

Sean was naked now; by contrast to the cook's luxurious curves, his body was firm and well-defined; his buttocks were so muscular as to look almost sculpted. Alison stared at his cock. The gross organ that had ravished her young pussy, then slid into her bottom and spewed its hot load, was limp now; it dangled in front of the slack, low-slung balls.

Hermione took her eyes off Rosie and scrutinised Sean. "What's the matter with that?" she asked, prodding his cock with the butt of her whip. "It wasn't all soft like that this afternoon when Rosie was sucking it off – was it?"

Alison drew in her breath. So that was what Hermione had caught them doing! She looked at Sean with a different expression. Didn't he *ever* have enough? He screwed me twice, once up my pussy, and once up my arse, this afternoon – and then he still wanted the cook to suck his cock off for him! She had to stifle the urge to giggle. No wonder his cock was soft and limp – it'd had a very busy day!

A cruel smile crossed Hermione's face. "Well have to see what we can do about that, won't we, Sean?"

Alison thought his face turned paler.

"All right," Hermione nodded to Rosie. "Bend over the stool!"

Reluctantly but obediently, Rosie went up to the strange stool and leaned her curvaceous body over it.

Alison watched as the fleshy buttocks spread open, and she thought she could see a trickle of wetness sliding down the insides of Rosie's thighs.

Hermione nodded to Alison. "Fasten her hands and feet to the legs of the stool with the straps."

Wonderingly, Alison did as she was asked, hearing Rosie groan when the leather thongs pulled her legs wider apart.

"Tighten the leather," Hermione

instructed. "I want her stretched as tight as a bow!"

Rosie's bottom moved up higher when Alison tightened the thongs on her wrists. She glanced at it, feeling a flicker of excitement when she caught a much closer glimpse of the puckered opening of Rosie's anal orifice. It looked well used, as if it were ready to accommodate any comers: she restrained a temptation to stick her own finger into the brown, pouting sphincter.

The cook's thighs parted more widely when Alison tightened the straps on her ankles, and the hairy tip of her vulva became more clearly visible. Alison had been right. Rosie's sex was lubricating heavily.

What, Alison wondered, are the other straps on the legs for?

Hermione answered her unspoken question.

"Position yourself behind Rosie, Sean!"

The chauffeur stumbled forward and stood just inches behind the trembling bottom of the cook.

"Fasten two straps to Sean's ankles!" Hermione ordered.

The two straps were longer than the ones which held Rosie in place, and when Alison had, obediently, fastened them, Sean was still twelve inches or so behind the cook.

"Now take the long straps from the front of the stool and fasten them to Sean's hands," said Hermione.

Meekly, Sean held out his wrists and let Alison slip on the leather cuffs, tightening them so that he was standing, still upright, but stooped forward though not touching Rosie's naked body.

Hermione stared at the limp, dangling cock, then tapped it with her whip. "Your wonderful, hungry cock seems very quiet tonight, Sean!" she sneered.

He shivered. "I – I'm tired, Madam."

Alison restrained a smile. How could Hermione know that her chauffeur had raped her twice that afternoon?

Hermione stood so that she could talk into Sean's face. "I want you to screw Rosie's arse, Sean – I want you to stick your filthy cock right up her arsehole and fuck!" The words were spat out, viciously, and Sean recoiled.

"I... I can't, Ma'am, I can't!" he moaned.

The cruel smile came back to Hermione's face. "We'll see about that!"

Hermione hurried to her dresser, opened the bottom drawer and took out a small black box that made Alison's eyes open in wonder.

It was not unlike the box that Maurice had used that afternoon.

There was an electrical flex that Hermione plugged into a socket in the wall, and then she opened the box and took out a cable – with an electrode on the end.

"Doctor Maurice!" Alison gasped.

Hermione gave her a quick smile. "Something like that," she murmured and positioned herself behind the chauffeur, holding the electrode by its insulated end.

"Bend forward a little, Sean," she said, her voice dry with excitement.

"Ma'am," he protested, "please, Ma'am, not that!"

Hermione picked up her whip, then slashed him viciously across the buttocks. "Don't whinge!" She bent, chose her spot carefully then lashed between his parted legs, allowing the whip to cut across his scrotum. A scream of agony escaped from Sean's lips.

"Don't hurt him, Ma'am!" Rosie's voice, muffled, came from her hidden face.

"Keep your damned mouth shut," snarled Hermione. She changed her position, moving in front of Sean so that she was close to Rosie's exposed bottom. She raised the electrode, probing between Rosie's buttocks with the end of it until she found the opening to her vulva; viciously, she stuck the electrode in.

A wail started in Rosie's throat.

Hermione activated a switch and the electrode appeared to jerk in her hand. A high scream came from Rosie's lips and her buttocks writhed wildly. Hermione laughed and pressed the switch again. This time, Rosie's entire body lifted on the back of the stool; fierce shivers racked her flesh as shrill screams issued from her throat.

Alison watched as a stream of urine gushed down from the twitching vulva.

Hermione withdrew the electrode. "Just keep quiet, Rosie," she said, sounding calm, as though this sadistic act had appeased her anger.

"It's not the same type as Maurice uses," Hermione explained to Alison. "This one shocks instead of thrills; there's quite a difference, I can assure you," she laughed. She looked down at Rosie's shivering, urinating vulva. "Isn't that right, Rosie? It gives you quite a jolt, doesn't it?" But only babbling moans came from the cook's lips in reply.

Alison was surprised to find that her hand had slid underneath her baby-doll nightie; her fingers were between the lips of her pussy, gliding up, down, touching her clitoris, gliding down again. The erotic scene before her eyes was thrilling her intensely.

"Now, Sean," said Hermione, "you know what I'm going to do!"

He twisted his neck, showed a white face to his mistress, but kept his lips closed.

Hermione moved behind him again and hissed into the chauffeur's ear. "I want you to stick your cock in Rosie's arsehole and bugger her silly!"

The cook's large, creamy behind was open and vulnerable; the tan sphincter between her splayed buttocks was exposed and wickedly inviting, but Sean's cock remained soft.

Hermione squeezed the end of the electrode between Sean's buttocks, and then finding the chauffeur's own tight hole, thrust it in hard. He winced as the rod penetrated his anus but he managed to stifle his moans.

Hermione switched on the current and the tip of the electrode vibrated gently inside Sean's arse. Alison saw his penis tremble.

Hermione sent through a mild shock; Sean groaned this time but his cock twitched jerkily. She sent through a sharper shock. Sean screamed this time, but his cock moved upward and started to form an erection.

"Jam it in her arse, you fool," screamed Hermione. "Fuck her filthy hole, Sean, you damned fool!"

The end of his cock weaved as he took a shambling half-step forward; he staggered, half-fell and his cock squashed against

Rosie's bottom. He dragged himself upright – and Hermione sent through a fierce shock. He screamed, his body jerked and his cock slithered madly over Rosie's fleshy buttocks then jammed between the cheeks. As soon as Hermione saw its position, she sent through a massive jolt – and Sean screamed his agony, let his body lurch forward and his cock, swollen with artificial lust, tore through Rosie's anal flesh. Her screams blended with his and she flattened herself on the leather top of the stool. Sean teetered forward; Hermione jolted his arse again and his cock reacted, slamming in, pushing between the cheeks of the cook's abused bottom.

Alison had moved closer in her excitement; now, she was standing beside Hermione, who was weaving her own body in tune with the tortured writhings of Sean's and Rosie's violated bodies.

"Fuck her arse, Sean," Hermione shrilled, and Alison thought the crude words sounded curiously arousing in her cut-glass accent. Then the sadistic woman jolted him, sending a searing stab of electricity into his bottom. He screamed, jerked forward and felt his cock throbbing, expanding against the clinging flesh inside Rosie's abused arsehole.

"Stop!" he screamed suddenly. "Stop it, Ma'am, please stop!"

He was plunging his cock in and out of Rosie's jerking bottom without any help from the electrode. Rosie was squealing as the stiffened shaft was tearing in her very depths. "I – I'm coming, Ma'am," Sean sobbed, "I'm coming!"

Hermione sent a series of vicious shocks into his body, watching his bottom shaking and quivering as each successive jolt went in. Rosie's bottom looked like two quivering blancmanges, as the plunging cock pulled out wet flesh, then thrust it back in with each vicious lurch.

"Alison," howled Hermione, "help me... please help me!" She was standing with her legs astride, short leather skirt held high. "My pussy," she moaned into Alison's face, "please touch my pussy – I have to come!"

Hesitantly at first, then more boldly, Alison slid her hand between Hermione's thighs and moved her fingers up until she encountered warm, wet flesh that throbbed in her hand.

"Squeeze it, oh, please squeeze it, Alison, you sweet little girl!"

Hermione jerked her legs together, trapping Alison's hand.

A fresh shock stabbed into Sean's arse, and Hermione moaned with excitement. "Now, Alison, now!" Her voice rose, and

Alison moved her fingers rapidly as she felt Hermione's pussy squirming and convulsing on her hand as Hermione achieved a noisy climax.

The electrode was turned off; Hermione let the shaft slide from Sean's abused, tortured anus. He sagged down onto his haunches. Rosie lay on her face, sobbing, as Sean's thick lust-juice trickled out of her abused and wide-open anus.

"You darling," Hermione whispered to Alison as they stood close together behind the disciplined servants, "you sweet, lovable girl!" She turned her head, placed her hand behind Alison's head then kissed her on the lips. When Alison withdrew her hand from between Hermione's thighs it was soaked with her juices.

"Oh, Hermione, oh – " Alison quavered when the older woman withdrew her mouth from hers.

"Don't talk," whispered Hermione, stroking Alison's face. "It was all so beautiful, so special – especially you, you delicious darling thing; just don't talk... for now."

Hermione took a staggering step to her bed and sank down on the edge of it.

"Untie them," she said, her voice satiated, quiet; so different from the lust-crazed voice she had used when she was sending jolting shocks into Sean's arsehole and watching his cock tear into Rosie's anus. "I feel so tired," she smiled at Alison.

Alison unfastened the bonds while Hermione sat on the edge of her bed, rocking herself gently back and forth as she watched.

"Now, you can go," said Hermione to the servants. "Both of you – don't bother getting dressed here – take your clothes with you, and…" she took a deep breath, "I hope your taste of discipline has done you good."

They picked up their clothes with trembling hands and limped towards the door, Rosie wailing softly, deep in her throat, and Sean wincing each time one buttock pressed against the other.

Hermione smiled at Alison. "It was all so wonderful," she said again.

Alison smiled back at her; she was at such a high pitch of excitement that she was unable to speak. Now, she supposed, Hermione will do wonderful, exciting things to me – make me orgasm like I've never orgasmed, make me come like anything, blow, blast, squirt and rocket into cloud nine or ten or zillion!

But the young secretary was to be sorely disappointed!

"I feel quite drained," said Hermione, "emotionally and physically. Alison dear, I'd like to take you to bed with me, really I would, but it's not possible. Not tonight. Things affect me this way – take every little last drop of energy out of me. You do understand, don't you?"

Alison stared at her mistress, feeling her pussy contracting between her thighs. I don't understand! Her clitoris was stiff, peeping from under its hood, begging for attention. I want to orgasm, too! She squeezed one leg over the other and felt the residual waves of electricity vibrating in her body. The erotic scene had heightened, not lessened her overwhelming desire. I want a cock or a hand or understanding lips on my pussy and clit! That's what I understand – that's what I want!

Hermione's eyes were closing; a drowsy, satiated expression was relaxing the lines on her face. Alison gave her a sharp, bitter glance, then turned and stumbled out of the bedroom door. You bitch! You used me to make you come – just like you used Rosie and Sean's flesh – then you send me away when you're satisfied!

Alison walked blindly down the corridor until she came to her room. The roaring desire that possessed her body made her every movement unsteady. Her nipples were stiff, tortured tips of untouched longing and her pussy pleaded wetly with every pursing movement for sexual satisfaction. She pushed open the door, and staggered into her room, so engrossed with her own sensuous desires that she did not even notice that the light was already on.

"Hello Alison!"

The crisp greeting hit her like a bucket of cold water in the face. Greatly surprised, she stared at the figure who stood so defiantly, hands on hips, in the middle of her bedroom.

"My God, Jillian!" gasped Alison, more concerned about her own provocative state of near-nudity than the strange girl's appearance in her bedroom. "What on earth are you doing here?"

Jillian was dressed in men's stripy pyjamas. The top was left casually unbuttoned and Alison could see the nineteen-year-old's pert breasts and their puffy pink areolae. From the opening below the cord of her pyjama bottoms, a large artificial phallus protruded outwards and upwards. It was black and menacing, with a gloss to it that made it look more like a well-oiled torpedo than a penis. She held it delicately, between finger and thumb, pointing it at Alison's belly.

"I've come to fuck you silly!" she said, with an arrogant, superior grin.

Alison took a deep breath, reached behind her and slammed the bedroom door.

Chapter 9

The baby-doll nightie was tangled around Alison's neck; her legs were split in an impossible angle as she lay, spread-eagled, on her bed.

Jillian groaned as her slender torso writhed between Alison's wide-open thighs.

"Ooooh, Jillian," sighed Alison, "oooh yessss! Fuck me, oh, please *fuck* me…"

The massive dildo slid deeply inside her stretched-open pussy; each time she drove inward, Alison felt thrills vibrating on all parts of her vaginal walls; the thick shaft titillated her clitoris each time it dragged over it, making Alison draw in her belly then thrust up her pelvis to meet the next wave of delight.

"Urghh," grunted Jillian, "what a sweet, soft little cunt you have." She shoved her organ up to the top of Alison's sexual cavern, let it soak there for a few seconds, then dragged it slowly down. "God, look at that," she groaned, "look at the way your pink pussy-lips hug my cock! It's beautiful!"

Alison lifted her feet in the air, and felt her lesbian lover penetrate her even more deeply.

The twisting, writhing snake was appeasing some of the screaming demands of her charged-up, electrified flesh.

Jillian jerked her body forward; as she did so, Alison's was buffeted by the slender lesbian's strong thrusts. She drove in remorselessly, pulled out, then drove in again with manic energy, often pausing to squeeze, lick or torment Alison's beautiful, pliant breasts.

"Alison, Alison, sweet little Alison! I just knew you would love fucking."

"Yesss," she replied passionately, feeling the sensuous throbs spiral from her vulva to her belly, "you're... it's... just like a man f... fucking me — only better!" She thought briefly of Jonathan, then drove her heels hard down into the firm bottom cheeks thrusting above her, and the short-haired lesbian reared up like a spurred horse and plunged deeper into her. Their sexes ground together, hot, wet and swollen. Alison felt Jillian's pert, perky breasts bore into her own creamy mammary glands. Their lust-stiffened nipples kissed and grazed.

"How do you like my cock?" panted Jillian. "It's my biggest — and my favourite!

Nine inches long and nearly two and a half in diameter. I bought it from a friend who brought it back from Germany!"

"Ummm," a delicious ripple of sensuality was rolling up Alison's thighs and blending and blasting at the apex. "Oh, yes, Jillian – your cock's divine! And you're fucking me... better than my boyfriend ever did!" She sighed, felt herself filled to capacity, "With your lovely, big cock!" she breathed.

"Oh, Alison – I – I'm going to come soon!" Her movements became more frenzied and Alison's body responded; she, too, felt her orgasm nearing. "My, I'm going to squirt all over your cunt and make it all gooey, Alison, all hot!"

"Oooooh, Jillian – *yessss please*!" Alison squealed; it seemed as though the huge organ were swelling inside her, causing her sexual slot to hug it even more tightly. "I'm coming, Jillian, I'm coming, too!" screamed Alison.

Alison gripped her with her legs, entwining them round her lithe body; pressing her pelvis up, hungrily, increasing the contact between her gyrating clitoris and the vast, jerking penis. "*Eeeeagh! Jillian*," she screamed, "fuck – keep fucking me – please don't stop!" Her fingernails raked her back as she threw her arms around in a frenzy. Her bottom pressed into the bed, bouncing up against the lesbian's writhing body. Jillian drew grating gasps of air into her lungs, then groped below the huge organ to find the rubber scrotum, which she had carefully filled with milk and gelatine. She squeezed the little reservoir and her dildo started to spit its load. "Now – take all my cream, Alison, all my hot, fucking cream!"

She howled like an animal as she spurted the thick load into Alison's undulating pussy. In response the new secretary's head jerked up, her mouth opened, closed – then her teeth sank into Jillian's shoulder.

"Coming, ohhh!" she groaned, writhing herself wildly, "Oh, my God – I'm exploding inside my cunt! My clit's on fire!"

Their bodies twisted, climaxed and locked together on the bed in a pool of sweat and vaginal juices; gradually, their sensual gyrations reduced in intensity.

Alison turned her head and pressed her cheek into the pillow. Jillian's 'cock' was still inside her; now it was sliding slowly out of her ravaged pussy.

"That was good, Jillian," she whispered. "I came and it was very, very good!"

"Dear Alison," she said, "dear, sweet Alison. How did you like being flooded with my 'spunk'? Were you expecting something like that?" She reached up and touched

Alison's face tenderly, as though she were a china doll.

"It was wonderful," admitted Alison.

"It was really nice for me too," she said, tenderly. "You have such a nice little cunt – it was just made for fucking." She sighed then startled Alison by adding: "It was even as nice as the time I did it with Mummy!"

* * *

Alison lay on her face, not sure whether she had heard the girl correctly – dildo sex with her mother? Impossible. Her baby-doll nightie was still around her neck as Jillian sat up beside her, touching her skin, stroking, caressing, gently, delicately. She stared at her bottom then drew her fingertip up the sensuous cleft.

"Such a nice little arse," she sighed, squeezing the satiny cheeks.

"Be careful, Jillian," Alison said softly, "I'm rather sensitive down there just now."

"Nice and soft," she said, prying open the cheeks with her strong fingers, "and with a sweet, little, brown arsehole!" She leaned over her, staring at her anal hole.

Alison thought about what she'd said, and then asked, "Do you do it with your Mummy often?" trying to sound as casual as she could.

Jillian coughed, then said, "Yes, quite often. But it's sort of a secret. At least Mummy would be furious if she found out that I'd told you!"

"Have you done it with Hermione recently?" Alison whispered, still a little shell-shocked by the announcement.

Jillian lifted her hand, slapped her bottom lightly and laughed. "Hey! You shouldn't say that sort of thing. It's not really very nice to have sex with your own mother, is it?"

"But you do, don't you?"

Jillian laughed again. "Yes, we did it before dinner, sort of. Well, she brought me off with another dildo in the dining-room. It was so good I even squirted all over the carpet!"

Alison kept her face hidden in the pillow. "How long have you been doing this?"

Jillian cocked her head to one side, thinking. "Oh, I dunno! Almost three years, I think." She touched Alison's buttocks again, more roughly this time, pulling the soft, resilient cheeks apart and again exposing her anus. "Come on... let me fuck you again. You're the one I want to fuck now, not my scrawny old mother!"

Alison felt a flicker of surprise. What sort of lesbian nymphomaniac is this girl? Her own mother!

Her pussy reacted sensually to the thought, and she felt her clitoris twitch. The thick juice was still trickling out of her vulva, making it feel sticky and causing the lips to cling together each time she wriggled herself. She wriggled herself now.

"Wait until I turn over," she said, huskily.

"No!" Jillian pressed a heavy hand on her bottom. "Stay there – I'll fuck you like that!"

Alison wriggled, frantically. *Having Sean stick his cock up my arse is one thing... But Jillian – Jillian and this monstrous organ is something else! She'd split me open like a walnut!*

"No, Jillian," she mumbled, desperately squirming, "I don't want it like that – it'll hurt my bottom too much."

But Jillian continued to hold her in a prone position without any effort.

"Not up your arse, silly – up your cunt from the back!"

"Oh," she relaxed a little. "Oh, that!"

Jillian manoeuvred herself between her thighs as Alison spread them open. She raised her buttocks, dragging her knees up the bed, crouching so that the mouth of her vulva was high. She felt a little exposed and vulnerable in this position – as if she were presenting her genitals for the world to see and comment upon.

Jillian pressed her body against her and she could feel her warm breath hitting the back of her neck. The thick thatch of hairs that formed Jillian's pubic bush at the base of her belly tickled the cheeks of Alison's bottom as she thrust herself back against the invading rod.

Somehow the head of the strap-on dildo felt bigger now, thicker and hotter as it was inserted between Alison's open vaginal lips; but her pussy felt bigger, too, stretched open wider as she crouched in her waiting position.

"Now!" She drove in with all her strength and Alison felt her body shoved forwards. She pushed back with her hips felt Jillian thrusting in deeper, so she rotated her hips and bottom. Deliciously, the huge dildo throbbed against all parts of her pussy. She reached under herself, spreading her lips open with her fingers so that her clitoris could slide out, then she pressed her erect, throbbing flesh flush against the black rubber shaft as it ploughed in and out; the vibrating sensation was delicious.

"Oh, Jillian," she purred, "that's so nice!"

Her nipples felt like daggers of desire so she ground them into the bed, leaning herself down from the waist and rotating her body.

Jillian now leaned heavily on her back; she felt her hands go under her, slide high, find her breasts and start to maul them clumsily.

"Not like that," she whispered. "Tickle my nipples first!"

"Mmm... I love your tits," said Jillian huskily, searching for the stiff tips then squeezing them. "I'm going to pull on them, now!"

"Oh, yes," she sighed, "please do that!"

She strained herself backward to increase the tension on her nipples, and then, intuitively, Jillian gripped them harder.

Her strap-on was jerking erratically now. "I'm going to come soon, Alison, I'm so close now!" she panted.

Alison pressed her fingers down harder, jamming her clitoris against the relentlessly plunging cock. "Oh, yes, Jillian, me too!" she groaned.

It felt so deep inside her pussy that she imagined Jillian was probing in her belly. "Now," she said suddenly, urgently, pushing back with all her strength, "I'm coming now – push in deep, Jillian, fuck me really hard and deep!"

"Ohh, Alison... !" The beautiful lesbian girl rocked herself wildly, making Alison's body jerk up the bed then wriggle down again. Alison parted her knees to make the opening bigger to accommodate the width.

"Yesss!" she hissed, as she was overtaken violently by the continual spasms of her massive climax. "Yesss, Jillian!" Her legs straightened as Jillian squirted her feminine ejaculate all over her bottom, and Alison, too, gushed a small quantity of liquid that coursed down the insides of her thighs.

"That was fucking good," she sighed, "such a lovely cunt, Alison!"

She smiled, feeling tired but satiated. Her desire was appeased at last. "Fucking good fuck, Jillian," she murmured dreamily, "and you use that cock rather well!"

As Alison turned over she felt the remains of a warm, thick fluid flowing out of her pussy and her body seemed to relax as it never had before. Her eyes closed and drowsily she wondered if this had all been just another of those wonderful sex-filled dreams...

* * *

Alison was sound asleep when Jillian rolled herself off her bed and dragged on her pyjamas. She gazed fondly for a moment at Alison who looked so peaceful, her thighs thrown carelessly apart in her sleep, pussy-lips unfurled and open with a thick residue of juice drying on her skin, then she moved to the door, clicked off the light and stepped into the corridor. After only a moment's hesitation, she moved in the direction of her mother's bedroom.

* * *

Hermione was lying on her back, in much the same position as Jillian had just left Alison; the bedroom light was still on, too.

Jillian closed the door behind her, moved into the room and looked at her mother. The attractive forty-five-year-old was still wearing the leather skirt that she had donned for her bizarre session of discipline, but it was rumpled around her waist now; her belly, pubic hair and vulva were all exposed to her daughter's view.

The leather boots were discarded at the bedside and the flimsy halter was dragged up, revealing breasts that were still firm and pointed with enlarged, dark red nipples.

Jillian sank down, heavily, on the foot of the bed. The slight movement wakened Hermione.

She blinked in the light, then recognised her. "Ah, Jillian."

"Yes, Mummy," she replied. "It's me."

Her eyes went from her mother's face to her breasts, then down across her belly to her sex; silently, she stared at the thick, pink, prominent labia.

"Well?" Hermione murmured.

She reluctantly tore her eyes away, and moistened her lips. "Mummy, I just fucked Alison! It was super!"

She smiled at her daughter. "I thought it would be, dear."

She stared at her mother in silence.

"Did you both enjoy it?" Hermione's voice was soft.

Jillian nodded, vigorously. "She has the prettiest cunt ever, and she really loves being fucked, Mummy."

Hermione looked closely into her face. "She didn't – " she searched for the word, "object, I mean, try and stop you, at all, did she?"

Jillian grinned, shaking her head. "It was just like you said it would be, Mummy, she was all ready!"

She wet her lips by sliding a suggestive tongue between them. "It was amazing – when she came in and saw me with my big black rubber cock, she just lay down on the bed, pulled up her baby-doll nightie, and said – 'fuck me'!"

"Just like that!" Hermione raised her immaculate eyebrows.

"Well, Mummy – maybe not just like that, but as near as damn!"

Hermione smiled. "I know what you

mean, dear. She was all ready."

"Yes, Mummy, she certainly was. Her cunt was soaking wet."

Hermione smiled at her and she gave her mother a sheepish smile back. After a minute, she bent her head and kissed her bare feet.

Hermione sighed. "You're a dear girl, Jillian."

Her tongue slid out and she licked the insides of her mother's legs. The older woman sighed again, changing her position.

Jillian's head moved higher; she tickled the flesh behind and above her mother's knees with the tip of her tongue.

"Oh, Jillian," Hermione sighed once more, "do you like doing that?"

She lifted her mouth off her mother's flesh and grinned. "Yes, Mummy. You know I do!" Her head went down again.

Hermione leaned back, pressing her head into the softness of the pillow as the wet tongue snaked up her body.

"Mummy!" Jillian had stopped licking. "I want to stay here all night, if that's alright with you."

Hermione's lips moved. "Oh, Jillian, dear, I'm not sure…" she murmured.

"Can't I, Mummy? Can't I lie between your legs and suck your lovely cunt all night?" Her voice was hoarse and thick with desire.

Hermione opened her eyes, looking down her body until she met her handsome daughter's eyes. She was staring at her with such an eager, beseeching look that Hermione's heart melted.

She nodded.

"Very well, Jillian," she whispered. "Lock the door and turn out the light, then take off your pyjamas." She smiled, a tender, maternal smile. "You can do what you want, darling. You can suck and lick my private parts the way you like and then, if you want to, you can fuck me with your big thing!" Unconsciously, she ran her tongue over her lips; she, too, was thirsty for love, hungry for sex and consumed with desire yet again.

Jillian scrambled off the bed, locked the door and turned off the light. Then she shrugged off her pyjamas and slipped on the harness of her monstrous black phallus. In the soft, dim light she could easily have been mistaken for a very handsome young lad with a huge erection bobbing and weaving between his thighs. She looked at it proudly, then at her mother, and a radiant smile lit up her face. "Nice cock, eh?" she quipped, her eyes flickering from her own body to her mother's. "Nice cunt, too!" Her mother laughed as Jillian squirmed herself into position between Hermione's wide-spread limbs.

But first the young girl buried her nose in the abundant pubic hair of her mother's sex, her tongue seeking out, and easily finding, the large, swollen clitoris, which she engulfed with her warm, wet mouth. Hermione gave a sharp little intake of breath, her thighs tensed and her head jerked up. Jillian started to suck on greedily on the prominent nub of flesh between her mother's legs.

Hermione slowly let out her breath, opened her thighs a little wider, then felt herself drifting into a hazy, sensuous dream-world of incessant physical gratification as the gentle thrills throbbed up her body. She reached down and ran her fingers through the short crop of her daughter's thick, soft hair.

Chapter 10

Alison opened her eyes, blinking sleepily. Someone was tapping at her bedroom door. "Come in," she murmured, drowsily.

As the door opened, Alison glanced down at herself. Her baby-doll nightie was still around her neck as she lay on her back. She made a half-hearted effort to drag a sheet over her nakedness then lay back, limply, when she recognised Rosie.

The cook was carrying a small tray with a cup and saucer, sugar and cream on it. "I've brought you coffee, Miss," Rosie mumbled, putting the tray down beside the bed.

Alison glanced at her face with some concern. Her eyes were puffed and swollen as though she'd been crying, and her skin was white with red blotches.

Despite herself, Alison asked the unnecessary question. "Did Hermione hurt you last night?"

Rosie's voice was bitter. "Yes, you saw it!" A hard edge came into her tone, "It hurts to be tortured with electric shocks then – then have a hard thing stuck in – into you!" She looked at Alison coldly, then asked, viciously, "Did you enjoy watching, Miss – did you get your climax like Madam, too?"

"No!" Alison snapped, feeling angry. "Don't blame me for what happened to you. Your employer was punishing you for something you'd done!"

The spirit sagged out of the cook. "Yes, Miss. I'm sorry, Miss." She turned to the door and asked, "Is there anything else you'd like?"

Alison started to shake her head, then changed her mind. "Yes, tell Sean I want to see him."

Rosie looked startled. "Now? Here?"

"Yes," said Alison, putting sugar and cream into her coffee then sipping it, "see to it right away, please."

The venom came back into Rosie's face. "Yes, Miss," she almost spat, then exited.

Alison tensed then relaxed her belly; the muscles felt sore. *Jillian and her long thick dildo poking up into me! She must have reached all the way to my belly-button!*

She probed, delicately, between her thighs. The lips of her vulva felt tender; she caressed them very gently. The inside of her pussy was sore. *That huge cock must have stretched me! I've never had anything that big in me before!*

Alison's eyes flickered towards the dresser, where she had placed her array of body creams. *A soft, soothing cream up my pussy would be nice!*

There was a light tap at her door.

"Come in!"

Sean entered, hesitantly. "You wanted me, Miss Jeffreys?"

Alison had a crazy impulse to smile. *He always calls me Miss Jeffreys! Even when he's raping me he keeps calling me Miss Jeffreys!*

"Yes, Sean," she searched his face with her eyes. He didn't look hurt and abused like Rosie had. "Did you enjoy yourself last night?"

He winced. "I'm so sore, Miss Jeffreys," he wriggled, "all the way up – " he hesitated, then finished "my arsehole!" He gave her a wry grin.

"Serves you right," said Alison, smugly. "You had your fun with me in the afternoon – so you deserve what you got from Madam at night!"

He shook his head, then a worried expression crossed his face. "You – you didn't tell Madam about – you know, about what happened?"

"No," said Alison, slowly. "You said you'd do anything I wanted if I didn't tell her so I didn't!"

"Thank you, Miss Jeffreys," he murmured, dropping his eyes. "I meant what I said." He moved, uncomfortably; the young, vibrant flesh lying so nakedly on the bed was disturbing him.

Alison's hand moved down her body, and he followed it with his eyes.

"My pussy's very sore inside, Sean," Alison said, casually, touching the open vaginal lips with her fingertips.

"I – I'm sorry, Miss Jeffreys," he

muttered, hoarsely.

"Not just because of what you did to it," said Alison, meeting his eyes. "There was something else, too."

Sean took a jerky breath, and Alison saw a small movement at his crotch.

"I want you to push some soft, cool cream into my pussy, Sean, smear it all over and then," she moistened her lips, "suck it out of me with your mouth!" She finished in a whisper.

Sean's body stiffened, then he clutched at himself, gripping himself very tightly at the crotch. "Yesss, Miss Jeffreys," he hissed.

Alison jerked her head to the dresser. "The cream's over there, so get it!"

He moved jerkily across the room. "The big jar at the end," Alison told him.

He picked up the jar and moved to the bed, unscrewing the cap as he sank down.

Alison dragged a pillow down the bed, pushed it under her, then plunked her bottom down on it so that her pelvis was raised.

"Push it in really deep," she ordered, "then use your tongue to spread it around, all over my pussy and – and on my clit, don't forget my clit!"

"I won't forget," he promised, scooping a fingerful of cream from the jar.

Alison's hands slithered over her belly until

she was holding the lips of her vagina; carefully, she spread them open parting her thighs and bending her knees. Sean bent over the bed and stared into the pink opening; as the slit opened, the small clitoral nub became visible.

The hardness at his crotch increased and his lips became suddenly dry.

"Now," said Alison, "start creaming my pussy now!" She half-lifted her buttocks, pointing her pelvis at his face.

His finger trembled as he moved it to the tender, waiting flesh. Alison flinched slightly, when the cream-tipped finger touched her labia. "So cool!" she murmured.

He smeared it thoroughly, with loving care. Alison squirmed very gently as he touched the sensitive parts. Sean took a fresh scoop and ploughed it into the orifice; pushing it in deep, massaging the inner walls and each time he withdrew his finger, he dragged it upward so that it touched the stiffening clitoris and Alison would let out air, twitching her belly.

"Now fill it," Alison slurred when he had smeared cream for several minutes. "Fill my pussy completely; use all the cream you want – use all of it, push it all inside me – then suck it all out!" She hissed the last words, and Sean saw her mouth open slightly and her tongue quickly, lasciviously, brush the underside of her top lip.

He filled the palm of his hand with cream then squashed it against Alison's pussy, pushing it all up.

"Yes. Like that," she whispered, lifting her buttocks, making the vaginal opening larger. "Right in!"

He repeated the process until the vulva was overflowing.

"Smear it over my clit!" Alison hissed.

He did as she asked, and she jerked her body. "Do it again!"

His finger circled the stiff, oily little protuberance, causing it to bend this way and that.

"Oh yes. Do it. Just like that..." moaned Alison, "that is wonderful!" She screwed her eyes shut and moved her lips as though she was chewing.

Suddenly, Alison lifted her legs in the air; exposing soft, white buttocks then reaching under herself, pulling the cheeks apart until the brown orifice of her anus appeared.

"Shove some cream up there, too!" she muttered, her voice lower.

Sean's hand trembled as he smeared cream on it; gently, he pushed a creamy fingertip into the tight hole.

"In deep!" Alison said huskily, lifting her legs higher, "then suck it all out!"

Her eyes opened, and she stared between her up-raised legs at Sean's startled face. "You fucked it," she told him, "so you can suck it, too!"

The colour drained from Sean's face, then he started to lower his head onto the bed. "D'you want me to suck it out of your pussy first, Miss Jeffreys, or out of your arse?" he mumbled. "Suck my arse!" she sneered.

He lifted his head, turned his face to hers. "You'll have to turn over, Miss Jeffreys – lie on your face. I can't suck the cream out of your arsehole when you're lying on your back!"

There was a whirl of flashing white flesh and Alison lay on her face, buttocks protruding, thighs slightly parted. "Like that?"

Sean pressed his face against her bottom. "Like that is perfect," he sighed, whereupon his tongue slid out, found the tight, creamy hole and licked it, sucked it and dragged out a mouthful of cream.

"Uuum, Sean, that's nice!" Alison drooled, squirming her buttocks against his face. "Push your tongue in deeper!"

He took a gulp of air then pressed his mouth on her anus again. The tiny hole seemed to open and close under the touch of his tongue; he drew out cream, felt it dribbling down his throat and gagged, moving his mouth off her flesh.

"Don't stop!" she snapped. "Go on! Keep sucking!"

He forced his lips down again, squeezing his tongue into the narrow canal, tasting slightly greasy cream, saltiness and a familiar female flavour.

"Like that," she whispered. "Keep doing it like that!"

The anal lips pursed open under the manipulations of his tongue; Alison pressed her body back and moved her buttocks from side to side with slow, sensuous movements.

Suddenly Alison panted; air hissed from her mouth, then she gasped, "I – I'm getting a feeling that – that I've never had before!" She pressed up with her bottom, down with her breasts – then writhed.

Sean could feel the tiny arsehole throbbing under his tongue; then it squeezed closed, Alison gasped again, pushed back and the opening became wide. He sank his tongue into the mushiness as far as he could and Alison jerked. "It's like coming, Sean – like coming in my botty!" She jerked again, panted for air, then wrenched her bottom away from Sean's mouth and twisted herself onto her back. "Now, my pussy," she commanded, urgently. "Suck my pussy!"

Her pelvis lifted and lowered, slowly and temptingly, in front of his eyes. Sean flattened his lips against the cream-filled pussy; tasted the thick creaminess again, sank his tongue into it and started to suck the gooey stuff out.

"Oooohh, yes, like that," Alison moaned, writhing slowly from side to side.

"It's beginning to soothe the soreness out of my pussy – making the ache go away."

Sean swallowed cream, sucked out another mouthful, swallowed again. The vaginal flesh seemed to throb beneath his lips.

"My clitoris, too," said Alison. "Don't forget to suck that!"

He ran his tongue up the slit, touched the stiff little pinnacle, teased it, nibbled it and then sucked off its creamy coating.

"Do that again," Alison groaned. "Just like you just did on my clit!"

He repeated the sensuous action and Alison made a panting sound. "I'm going to come, Sean – keep on doing that – it's making me come. Ohhh, Sean, I'm orgasm – orgasming – *oohh*!"

Her clitoris weaved like quicksilver as he gripped it with his teeth; his tongue moved, tickling the tiny tip, exciting it and arousing it to new heights of sensuality.

"Ohhh, Sean – *Ohhh*!" Alison panted; twisting herself frantically, almost dislodging Sean's grip on her clitoris, then she let herself shiver and shake as her orgasm shattered through her flesh, spiralling from her blasting clitoris to the walls of her pussy, undulating, throbbing then arcing into her belly.

Slowly, tiredly, Sean withdrew his face from her body. She writhed, the movements gradually slowing down, then she opened her eyes, which she'd screwed shut as soon as her orgasm began, and smiled at him.

"That was nice, Sean, really very nice!"

She stretched herself luxuriously.

"Is that all, Miss Jeffreys?" he asked, huskily, his eyes on her luscious body.

Alison stared at his face without speaking, and then her eyes went down to his crotch. "I suppose you're all hard!"

Sean nodded. "Yes, Miss Jeffreys."

"Let me see it," Alison said, casually. "Open your trousers!"

He tensed, then did as she ordered. His organ projected like a finger of desire.

"Um," murmured Alison, "your cock's all big and hard. Does looking at me make it get like that?"

"Yes," he groaned.

"You like having it sucked," Alison

murmured, "that's what Mrs. Simpson caught Rosie doing to you yesterday."

"Yes," he mumbled guiltily, reddening.

Alison drew her finger up the slit of her pussy, then asked, "Is that what you like best? Having your cock sucked?"

Sean swallowed, then shook his head.

"Fucking?" she asked with raised eyebrows.

He nodded. "You, Miss Jeffreys, fucking you!"

She smiled at the compliment, then asked, "Why?"

Sean's mouth worked with his emotion. "Because, Miss Jeffreys, you've got the tightest, snuggest little cunt that I've ever fucked!" His penis reared as he spoke.

Alison smiled again, then her expression became quizzical as she remembered the night before and Jillian... Jillian and her monstrous cock! She wondered: is my pussy still snug and tight?

She looked at Sean's face; his expression was tense and strained. There's one way I can find out!

Her hands slithered down her body as her thighs parted, hugely. Her fingertips pulled on the lips at the top of the slit so that her clitoris oozed out. "All right," she said, her voice now very low, "fuck it!"

Sean trembled as he dragged down his clothes, then he staggered to the bed and dropped onto it, covering Alison's small, voluptuous body with his.

She reached down and touched his balls, squeezing them gently through their thick scrotal sack; she imagined she felt a churning movement inside as though there were a motor or an engine at work. His shaft thickened and became even stiffer, then he thrust the head up, found the still-creamy lips and plunged in between them.

The air hissed from Alison's lungs as the throbbing cock drove up her pussy; she felt her vaginal walls clutching at the organ, caressing it as it careened up its sexual path.

"Sweet Mother of God!" Sean gasped, screwing inward, dragging out.

Her clitoris was still aroused and she pressed down with her pelvis so that she could delight in the delicious pressure of the stiff shaft gliding over her clitoral tip.

"I – I can't hold it, Miss Jeffreys," Sean sobbed. "You've got me so worked up I'll be shooting my spunk any moment now!"

My pussy can still grip and squeeze tightly! The thought flashed into Alison's mind as Sean pounded madly towards his orgasm. I've simply got to be small and tight if I can make his cock shoot off so fast! A

laugh rippled through Alison's belly, and the vibrations ran down to her clitoris, bringing on her own orgasm with unexpected rapidity.

"Ohhh, Sean, ohhh!" she squealed, climaxing, rocking herself and all the while feeling the hot blasts from his spitting, spurting cock inside the depths of her pussy.

"Miss Jeffreys," Sean gasped, "you're the best – the most brilliant, marvellous fuck in the world!" His exhausted body lay limply on top of Alison.

Slowly, Sean rolled off the body of his mistress – for that was what she was, now that he had to obey her every command.

"I – I suppose you want me to go, Miss Jeffreys," he mumbled.

She didn't answer him directly. "Well?" she said, questioningly.

He looked blank.

She squirmed with irritation. "Is it still snug and tight? My pussy, I mean!"

A slow smile spread across his face. "The snuggest, Miss Jeffreys, the tightest, sweetest fuck!"

She smiled back at him.

"I'm glad you're here," he said with sincerity. "I hope you're going to stay."

She nodded.

"Is there anything else you'd like, Miss Jeffreys?" he asked, still smiling.

"Yes, there is," she surprised him by answering. "There's some massaging cream over on the dresser, and I'd like to be massaged all over. A real massage, I mean – not a sex massage – " she let her eyes smile at him. "You can rub it into the cheeks of my bottom, of course, and over my breasts, but not up my pussy or inside my botty, I just want a good massage. I take very good care of my body, Sean – very good care."

"It's a luscious little body," he mumbled.

"And I want to keep it that way," she murmured. "Now, will you massage me?"

He nodded and swallowed. It would always be a thrill just to move his hands over that delicious, firm-fleshed, fresh young body that excited him so wildly.

"Yes, Miss Jeffreys," he said, moving to the dresser and finding the cream she'd mentioned. "It'll be a pleasure to massage you any way you like – any time!"

He poured some lotion onto the palm of his hand then began to rub it onto her back.

Alison lay on her face, smiling, feeling pleasurably relaxed and utterly sexually fulfilled. The caressing, soothing motion of Sean's hands on her back was lulling her to sleep.

"Is that the right way, Miss Jeffreys?" Sean asked in his soothing Irish lilt, massaging soft cream into her even softer body. He sneaked a glance at his wristwatch: eleven o'clock! Downstairs, they'd be wondering what had happened to him. He grinned: Well, let them wonder – I don't care!

"Yes, Sean," said Alison, drowsily, answering him, "that's exactly the way that I like it!"

She liked what he was doing – and the way that he was doing it. Alison smiled: There are a lot of things I like about Lazonby – and then she wondered: When am I going to start work?

Chapter 11

Alison started to perform her duties at Lazonby soon after she'd finished her leisurely late breakfast.

Mrs. Simpson was still in her room, Rosie informed Alison as she served her bacon and eggs, sausages, fried tomatoes and mushrooms; young Jillian was nowhere to be seen.

Alison was sipping her second cup of coffee when Hermione came into the dining-room. "Good morning, Alison," she said quietly, smiling. "I hope you slept well."

Alison looked up at her employer; Hermione was neatly dressed in a smart tweed suit, hair carefully coiffed and face lightly made up. It was hard to connect this well-dressed, well-bred woman with the erotically sadistic female who had performed perverse acts upon the hapless bodies of her servants in her bedroom the night before.

"Good morning, Hermione," said Alison. "You look very well, very attractive."

"Thank you," Hermione laughed. "I've been lying in my tub for almost an hour; that always relaxes my body."

Alison smiled; there was no reason to tell Hermione what method she had used to obtain complete relaxation.

"You look as fresh and pretty as ever," Hermione sighed, enviously. "Are you ready to start work this afternoon?"

Alison laughed and finished her coffee. "I think it's about time."

Hermione rang the bell for Rosie and seated herself at the table. "I'll see you in the office at two," she told Alison, picking up her morning mail which Rosie had left on the table.

* * *

"And this is a list of the tenants," said Hermione, "with their address and monthly rent."

Alison peered over Hermione's shoulder at the handwritten list of names.

"Their houses all have names, not numbers," she murmured.

Hermione laughed. "This is Somerset countryside, dear. The houses and cottages are scattered all over – not neatly laid out in streets like in the city."

"How do they pay their rent, by cheque?"

"Some of them, but others are so old-fashioned that they like to pay in cash."

"Do they come to the Hall?" Alison asked.

Hermione shook her head firmly. "Never. We collect from them in person."

"You?" Alison looked at Hermione in surprise; she couldn't imagine this aloof woman knocking at cottage doors and collecting rents.

"Usually," said Hermione. "I used to send Jillian sometimes, but – " her eyes became vacant, "the dear girl always seemed to have problems..." she broke off, looking at Alison. "Where is that girl, by the way?"

"I haven't seen her at all today," said Alison, feeling herself blush as she remembered the sensuous episode in her bedroom the night before.

"Probably walking about the grounds," she sighed. "She loves the outdoors." She looked at the list of names again. "Well, Alison, it'll be your job to collect rents now – that's one of your duties here. Let me see," she scanned the list, "you can walk over to Mr McEwen's cottage this afternoon; he always pays in cash and his rent's due right now."

Alison looked at the address. "Rose Cottage," she read. "Where in the world is that?"

Hermione got to her feet and strolled to the window. "Look!" She pointed to the end of the gardens; there was a gap in the line of trees and three small hillocks were visible. "It's on the slope of the middle hillock," Hermione explained. "You can't see it from here; it's a small white cottage with a climbing rose growing up the side of it."

"What's he like?"

Hermione looked at Alison. "Max McEwen?" she laughed. "He's an elderly eccentric – lived at Rose for as long as I can remember."

"He lives alone?"

"Mostly," said Hermione, thoughtfully. "He has relatives and friends staying with him from time to time. Well," her tone became brisk, "you can walk over there, Alison; take this small receipt book, collect his rent, in cash, then come back." She smiled. "That'll be your work for today."

Alison smiled at her employer; it didn't sound like a big day's work.

* * *

The cottage was only a half-hour's walk from Lazonby, but Alison was glad that she was wearing sensible low-heeled shoes; in any case, they complimented her light, cotton skirt and cream blouse, which was all she needed on this pleasant, balmy day.

She approached the heavy oak door, looked vainly for a bell, then rapped on the wood.

Instead of the door opening, a voice called out loudly, "Who is it?"

"I – I'm from Lazonby," Alison called, nervously. "I've come to collect the rent."

"Then come in," the man's voice shouted. "The door's not locked!"

She turned the big handle, pushed and the door swung open, soundlessly. Alison stepped inside, staring about her nervously and curiously. The front door opened onto the main room, and in the centre of the floor, a frail, elderly man was sitting behind a large desk. The cottage's interior was well-furnished in a simple, old-fashioned way, with a predominance of books: books in bookcases, on shelves and even stacked up against the walls on the floor.

He fixed his eyes on Alison with a piercing stare. "You're someone new; I haven't seen you before!"

Alison approached him diffidently. "I – I've just started working for Mrs. Simpson; I'm going to be looking after the rents and things."

He smiled. "Well, now, you're a change from Hermione!" He drank her in with his eyes. "Pretty as a picture and soft as honey and cream," he murmured, as if to himself.

Alison smiled, flushed at the compliment.

He slid open a drawer, took out a small pile of bills, counted some off and put them on the desktop. "Here's the rent, Miss – " he paused, "you didn't tell me your name."

"Jeffreys," she said, "Alison Jeffreys."

He nodded, "You've got a pretty name, too." He waited, then said, "You'll have to come and get the money, you see, I'm paralysed."

Alison drew in her breath, noticing the crutches beside his desk for the first time. "I – I'm sorry," she mumbled, moving forward,

"I didn't know!" She picked up the money, counted it and pushed it into her small purse. "I'll give you a receipt."

"Don't be sorry," he said, "it's just my legs. The rest of me's all right." He laughed. "I get around; you'd be surprised how I get around."

Alison moved beside him, bent over his desk to make out the receipt then felt his hand on the bare flesh of her leg at the back, just underneath her skirt. She flushed and squirmed herself slightly, but went on filling in the amount on the receipt.

"Nice, firm, young flesh," the old man murmured, stroking the roll of flesh on her inner thigh.

Alison squeezed her legs together. "Mr McEwen – please!"

His hand went on moving, sliding up her thigh all the way to her silken panties. "Max," he said, "everyone calls me Max!" His finger moved inside the tight leg of her panties and he stroked the crevice of flesh where the swell of her buttock met the top of her thigh.

"Don't," Alison whispered. "Really, Mr McEwen – it's not right!"

The drawer in his desk was still open; he reached in with his free hand, took out a note and pushed it across the desk to Alison. "A small gift for you," he said, softly. "Does that make it right?"

A fresh flood of colour suffused Alison's face. She stared at the note and saw that it was a fiver!

His hand was on the back of her panties, where they stretched so tightly across her bottom. He drew his finger up the silk-covered cleft. "Take them off," he whispered. "I just want to stroke it, caress it and feel it!"

Alison stood very still, staring at the five-pound note and trying to think straight. He isn't hurting me! But this is so...

"I'm just an old man," murmured Max McEwen. "I'm here by myself most of the time – I don't get much fun!"

His hand was high under her short skirt, pulling at the waistband of her briefs, sliding them down her legs.

Alison squeezed the cheeks of her bottom tightly together to impede him. He felt the muscular contraction. "Don't do that," he pleaded. He reached in the drawer again and took out two more notes, placing them with the first.

Another ten, Alison saw. Her buttocks relaxed and her panties slid down to her ankles.

He squeezed the soft flesh with lecherous pleasure. "Sweet little bottom," he mumbled, "as nice as I've ever felt!" His finger slithered through the cleft, touching the small anal orifice, lingering a moment then moving on. "Lean over the desk," he murmured, his voice shaky. "I want to see it as well as touch it. Bend forward, Alison, let me look at your lovely wee arse!"

Her face was burning but Alison leaned forward, propping her chin on her hands as she leaned over the wide desk, letting her bare, rounded bottom project just inches from the old man's face.

He stroked the soft flesh lasciviously, making little liquid sounds of pleasure. He squeezed the pliable rolls on either side of the cleft with jerky, excited movements. His hand slid lower, touched the crevice at the top of her thigh – then moved inward.

"No!" Alison tensed herself. "No! Not there – you never said that you'd touch me there!"

His fingertip found the wet lips at the entrance to her vagina, and tried to slide in. Alison tightened the cheeks of her bottom, squeezed her thighs together and his finger was trapped.

"Go on, lassie!" he panted, struggling to move his finger. "Let me feel inside your cunt!"

"No!" Alison moaned, gritting her teeth, jamming her buttocks together.

"Just – just my bum – you said you wanted to touch my bum – not my... my pussy!"

"Here," he gasped, breathlessly, "have this – and this – and this!" His hand shook as he reached in the desk-drawer, took out notes and added them to the three in front of Alison.

She twisted her head down and watched in wonder. One, two, three, four, five... She gasped; there must be seven or eight notes by now – and all fivers!

She relaxed her buttocks, parted her thighs and waited breathlessly for his reaction.

His hand had moved off her flesh; he was doing something that she couldn't see, in his lap. She could hear the rustle of clothing, then he spoke. "Now do what I want – any damned thing I want!"

Alison screwed shut her eyes. He's paid me! "But don't hurt me!" she pleaded.

"I won't hurt," he promised. "Stand up and turn around!"

Startled, Alison did as he asked, then tried to stifle a gasp of astonishment. He had unfastened his trousers at the front; now a long, slim penis projected straight up as he slouched back in his armless chair.

He grinned at her expression. "Squeeze your wet cunt onto that!"

Alison felt a crazy blend of fear and fascination.

The old man reached to her skirt and dragged it up at the front, staring at her pubic thatch.

"Brunette," he mumbled. "I like brown hairs round a young, juicy cunt!" He licked at his lips, then mumbled, "My granddaughter's a brunette!"

"Your *granddaughter*!" Now Alison's voice was shocked.

He nodded. "As pretty a little sixteen-year-old as you ever saw."

Alison's mouth sagged. "You – you do this to your granddaughter?"

He gave a cackling laugh. "Every month when she comes to see her poor old grandfather." He wet his lips. "She's got the tightest little cunt I ever fucked!" His penis twitched as he spoke.

Alison stared at him in horror. "You're a monster!" Her eyes were round, angry. "Doing that to such a girl – you awful creature!"

He cackled again, and then made his voice wheedling. "What else can a lonely old man do?"

"You – you – " Alison broke off and

sighed. He's a lecherous, incestuous old man, taking advantage of a young innocent girl and now, trying to do the same thing to me! She moved her lips indignantly, but then had a crazy impulse to smile. He pretended to be so helpless, sitting paralysed in his chair, but he'd managed to find a way to get his erotic thrills by doing awful, sensuous things to juicy, young girls, he said! She sighed again. He has some kind of courage – and determination... and, he's paid for his fun!

"Now, take your skirt off," he said, impatiently. "Step out of those cute little panties and straddle me with your sexy young thighs – as you can see – I have a mind to fuck!" He gripped his penis at the base, and Alison saw the head swell. "My cock's all ready," he rasped. He met Alison's eyes, adding, "And I've paid for it!"

Slowly, averting her eyes, Alison unclasped her skirt and dropped it on the desktop; daintily, she stepped out of her panties and took a nervous step toward the old man in the chair.

He stared at her belly and thighs as she got closer to him; there was a sheen of sweat on her skin, making it glisten and appear more sensuous, erotic, desirable.

He wet his lips, reached forward, gripped

her round the buttocks and pulled her closer, burying his nose in her soft pubic bush.

"You'll have to do it all," he told her. "As I told you – I don't have the use of my legs." He watched as involuntary ripples ran across her belly and her thick pubic thatch seemed to bristle with electricity.

Alison felt herself trembling, more with anticipation than fear. The things that had been done to her – that had happened to her – in the last few days were keeping her body in a constant state of sexual arousal. Just the sight of the slim cock waiting to penetrate her pussy was exciting her anew.

"Stand with your legs on either side of me," he instructed, his voice hoarse with excitement. "Then lower your bottom until your cunt's over my cock, and then – " he took a wheezing breath, "jam it down, all the way down, on my cock!"

Alison shivered as she took a jerky step into position, moving awkwardly, with her feet apart, inching herself forward, one leg on either side of his. He moved his hand down, under her crotch, fumbling at her wet vaginal lips. She jerked and made a low sound as she felt his cock-head brush against her slit, the muscles in her thighs aching as she held them in this unnatural position.

"Now, let your cunt slide down!" he panted.

She bent her knees, feeling her legs trembling and lowered herself slowly. He gripped her buttocks and guided her until she was over his cock. Her pussy felt stretched open, her belly stiff and strained as her body went down.

"Ohhhh!" A long sigh of delight escaped his lips as her vaginal lips opened on the head of his cock, letting the organ slide inside. "Press down," he groaned.

She relaxed her legs; her cunt slid lower, enveloping the stiff, slim cock completely.

"Oh, my, that's good," he sighed.

"Now, you'll have to move up and down – I – I can't help you, Alison; you'll have to glide your cunt on and off my cock. Just bend then straighten your legs!"

The breath panted from Alison's lips as she started to do as he asked. It was a new and strangely delicious feeling to be able to grip his stiff cock with her pussy, moving it as fast or as slowly as she liked. She rotated her bottom gently, squirming her pussy from side to side, letting the long, straight cock touch all the special spots inside her bubbling cunt. "Ohhh," she groaned, "oh, ohhh yesss!"

He lay back in his chair with his eyes closed and a tense, excited expression on his face. He let a smile cross his lips when he heard Alison softly groan. "You like it," he whispered. "It's different, isn't it, Alison – it's nice!"

"Ohhh," she moaned, raising herself slowly, feeling the cock sliding against the sides of her sucking pussy, "so new!"

Next time she pressed herself down, Alison leaned forward, her face moving close to the old man in the chair, as she forced her clitoris to make contact with his stiff, throbbing but unmoving cock; the erotic friction raised her to a new height of excitement.

"I – I can't move my cock," he gasped, "but I can play with your nipples if – if you'd like it!"

Her breathing became ragged as she felt spasms rippling from her clitoris to her pussy; she rubbed herself with increasing urgency against his shaft, then she moved her hand from the back of his chair, where she'd placed it to steady herself during her sexual exercise, and groped at the front of her blouse.

He helped her to unbutton it, and then cupped her bra-less breasts with trembling hands. "Sweet, luscious tits," he murmured as he kneaded them in his hands. Then, forcing his head forward and taking a nipple between his lips, he sucked at it hungrily as Alison raised and lowered her body, increasing then decreasing the tension on the stiffening tip of her nipple.

"That," she hissed. "Ohhh, that's so goood!"

The muscles in her thighs were beginning to ache from her strained position and constant raising and lowering action, but the thrills, running from her nipple to her clitoris then spiralling inside her belly, were making her throat contract with sexual excitement. This was different, thrilling and excitingly new!

He let his mouth slip off her nipple. "How d'you like it?" he asked in a hoarse whisper. "I'm not fucking you, Alison, girl – you're fucking me!"

A ripple of excited laughter ran through his body and Alison felt his cock swelling, swelling!

"I – I'm going to come, Alison," he gasped. "Your tight little pussy is hugging my cock so snug that I – I – Alison, *urgh – urgh*!"

She jammed her body forward and felt the swollen organ gyrating against her clitoris. His mouth groped, blindly, for her nipple, found it and bit. She squealed at the sudden pain, feeling her orgasm starting.

"Ohhh, my pussy," she gasped, "my clit –

ooh – my breast!" She shook her whole body, wildly, pressed down with all her strength and felt the head of the cock jam against the top of her pussy, jerk, spurt and explode.

"All over me," she squealed as she climaxed, opening and closing her legs spasmodically, bending and straightening her knees. "Right up my cunt, all wet, all hot, *ohh*!" Her buttocks contracted, opened, jammed closed again and the walls of her vulva sucked at the jerking, spurting cock until all the juice was spent.

The old man sank back in his chair; his lips slid off Alison's sensitive, bitten nipple. "You're a juicy, young cunt," he mumbled in appreciation. "You're a sweet, tight fuck, too – you've the sexiest cunt of the lot!"

Alison rested her cheek against the top of his head, still straddling him, her legs limp now, as the warm wetness slid down from inside her pussy and pooled at the base of his softening cock. She dragged in a gulp of air and said, "I've never done that – anything just like that – before!"

He reached behind her and stroked her sweating bottom. "But you'll do it again – " he smiled, confidently. "At least once a month – probably more, Alison – so much more!"

She drew her head back, looking into his face. "I – I don't know," she murmured. She turned and saw the small pile of notes on his desk. She thought: it was different and thrilling and wonderful – and he paid me for it, too!

"You'll come again, won't you?" he asked.

She giggled at the unintentional pun, and then blushed. "I'll have to collect the rent each month, anyway," she admitted.

"Maybe I'll start paying weekly," he said with a smile.

She laughed. Such an old devil!

His face became serious. "I want you to come and see me at least once a week, will you?" He glanced at the open drawer with the pile of notes in it. "You won't be sorry," he added, softly.

She blushed again. It wasn't just the money...

"All right," Alison said, "but not just because of that." She nodded to the open drawer. "But because you're a lonely old man with nobody to help you except, maybe, your granddaughter, and... who else?" She looked at him with raised eyebrows.

He gave her a sheepish grin. "My – my niece – my young niece!"

Alison drew in her breath. "You old rogue!" She tried to look shocked. "Has she got a nice, tight pussy, too?"

"No nicer than yours," he assured her, stroking her bare bottom.

"You're the best, Alison – the sweet, fucking best of the bunch!"

"What a thing to say," she protested, but she didn't really mind his words. Far from it, in fact, she found them flattering. "And who else is there?"

He shook his head, didn't answer.

Suddenly, a thought occurred to Alison. "Who used to collect your rent?"

"Hermione or Jillian," he muttered.

"Jillian?" Alison sounded surprised.

He nodded. "Aye, the stupid girl – can't do anything right!"

Alison was quiet, thinking about the previous night. She wasn't so sure that Jillian couldn't do anything right!

"What about Hermione?" she asked, curiously.

He shifted uncomfortably in his seat. "Let's not talk about her. I'm glad you're here, Alison, and that I'll be seeing you often."

Alison lifted herself. His limp cock was still inside her pussy; now, it slipped out, slowly and wetly.

"You've got a sopping wet pussy now, all right," he said, glancing down to watch the whitish fluid drip out of it.

"Your stuff," said Alison, edging herself back and reaching down for her panties, "– you shot it all into me."

He watched her take a dainty handkerchief from her tiny purse, wad it, and then wipe at her vaginal lips. "And very nice, too," he said. "Juicy cunt, luscious fuck!"

She pulled on her panties, then wrapped her skirt around her waist.

"I can suck you off if you'd like it sometime," he informed her. "D'you like having your pussy sucked?"

Alison dropped her eyes. "Maybe," she whispered, colouring a little, "but not now." She picked up the small pile of bills, stuffing them into her purse with the rent money. "I'd better be going – Hermione will wonder what I'm doing all this time." She gave an excited giggle.

"If she knew what an oversexed kitten you were, she wouldn't wonder," he said slowly.

"D'you think I'm oversexed, Mr McEw... Max, I mean?" Alison asked seriously.

"Definitely," he answered, "and I like it."

Alison was thoughtful. "I don't think I am, not really. It's just that so many things have been happening lately – "

He nodded, smiled knowingly. "I can believe that!"

Alison turned to the door. "I'll see you next month then, Max."

"I'm glad that you think you know me well enough to call me Max now." He grinned at her expression. "And I'll see you before next month – some time next week I hope!"

Alison looked doubtful.

"I'm always here," he added. "Please come, Alison; I'll be waiting – and looking forward to seeing you."

"I'll try," she promised, opening the door. "I'll try, Max," and she left.

She saw Jillian before Jillian saw her. She was standing behind a low azalea bush with only the top part of her body visible; her head was thrown back and she seemed to be staring at something in the sky.

"Jillian!" Alison called, moving toward her. "What are you doing here?"

It was only a few minutes since she'd left Max McEwen's cottage.

Jillian started, then a slow smile spread over her face when she saw Alison.

"Oh... A... Alison," she said with a slight stammer, "I – I was waiting for you."

"Waiting for me! But how did you know where I was?"

She grinned, slyly. "I saw you going to that old goat McEwen's house!"

"And you've been waiting all this time?" Alison glanced at her watch; she'd been inside that dirty old man's cottage for nearly an hour.

"What did you want to see me for?"

She licked her full lips nervously and moved out from behind the bush. "For a fuck," she said. "I wanted to fuck your cunt again, Alison!" And as Alison looked down, she could see the immense shaft projecting from her open jodhpurs. As before, the artificial cock was well oiled.

Alison's face paled. "But here – " she panted, her eyes flickering around them, "not here, Jillian!"

"Yes, here," she nodded, speaking slowly, with intensity, almost hypnotically, "let me do you on this nice soft grass, Alison, soft and smooth to lie on." She moved up to her and Alison took an instinctive step back. "Lie down, Alison – open your lovely legs and let me fuck you!"

"No, Jillian, no – I don't want to!" Alison blurted, moving back.

Her employer's daughter looked stricken and even a little angry. "Last night, Alison – last night you…"

"That was different," she cut in. "Don't think you can just grab hold of me whenever you feel like it," her breasts shook with indignation, "just because your 'cock' is always hard doesn't mean you can rape me when you like!"

Her face set in a stubborn expression. "I want to fuck," she said like a spoilt, peevish child, "yes, and if I want to fuck your cunt, Alison, I will!"

"No!" she snapped.

Jillian pushed at the older girl, almost causing her to fall. "You're my dolly," she said in the same childish voice, "and Mummy said I could fuck my dolly any time I liked!" She pushed again and this time Alison lost her balance and fell onto a grassy hillock on her back. Her skirt was around her waist and Jillian stared at the tightly stretched panties, still damp at the crotch. Her words had startled her. "Your mother said that?"

She was staring at her crotch. "Why – you're wet there, Alison – all wet!"

"What did your mother say?" she asked urgently.

She grinned. "Mummy said I can fuck you whenever I want to! She said you would be bound to like it... please let me... *please*..."

Alison's face flushed angrily. What do they think I am?

"Well, your precious Mummy's wrong!" she retorted.

Jillian dropped down beside her, and a long fingernail ripped at her panties, splitting them open at the crotch.

"No, Jillian, no!" Alison panted.

The predatory young lesbian pressed her hand into the opening, found Alison's saturated pussy and clawed inside it, clumsily, painfully.

"You're hurting me," she panted, wriggling out of her reach.

Jillian merely looked at her, breathing hard through her nose. "I need to fuck!" she hissed, chewing her lower lip.

"*No!*"

She rolled herself towards her with surprising speed; before Alison knew what she was going to do she had twisted her face down on the grass. She felt her lifting her skirt and felt the cool air on her bottom; then Jillian moved the torn panties off her buttocks and brought down her hand in a slap.

"Owww!" The startled gasp of pain shot from Alison's lips. She was startled as much as hurt.

The younger girl slapped down again and her hand sank into the soft flesh, leaving an angry red imprint on each quivering cheek.

"Don't," she moaned. "Owww, don't, Jillian, don't!"

She slapped again, watching her buttocks wriggling about and squirming, trying to get away. She spanked her bottom more viciously as her victim opened and closed her thighs in pain and frustration.

"Stop spanking me," she pleaded. "You're hurting my bottom!"

Jillian laughed. Then she said in the same irritatingly childish, sing-song voice, "You're my little dolly – and I can do what I like with my dolly – spank her if I like!"

She spanked her bottom again.

Frantically, Alison twisted her eyes sideways. Jillian was sitting beside her while she administered her punishment. Her artificial cock was huge, but from her previous experience of it, Alison knew that half of it extended inside its wearer. She watched it twitch each time Jillian's hand slapped onto her helpless flesh.

Stealthily, Alison stretched out her hand and touched the massive organ.

Jillian flinched, made a sound of surprise, then her hand spanked down onto Alison's red and throbbing bottom again.

Alison curled her fingers round the black rubber cock, jerking it in and out. "*Urgh*!" Jillian groaned deep in her throat and her legs seemed to tense. She slapped her bare skin again, but not so hard this time. Alison barely made a whimper – but her hand still pulled on the phallus. It was slimy with Jillian's secretions and her fingers glided gently up and down. Jillian pressed herself back and her shaft seemed to grow longer, thicker. Alison's fingers encircled its bulbous head and squeezed. The sight excited her; her hand moved more quickly.

Jillian spanked her again, but she was hardly aware of it. Her bottom was curiously deadened by the series of slaps it had received. Her attention was riveted on the throbbing organ within her hand. She squeezed, sliding the hidden half in and out of her tormentor. Jillian made an animal-like sound. Alison turned the head of the organ so that she was staring into the slitted lips in its head; it was so long that it seemed only inches from her face. She massaged it, watching the lips spew open, squeeze closed, then open again. A sound of pleasure oozed from Jillian's throat and her hand rested on a cheek of Alison's bottom, not moving, not spanking any more.

She massaged Jillian's cock sensuously; slowly then quickly, hearing the grating sobs pant from her throat.

"Urgh, Alison," she gasped, "urgh, Alison!"

Her hand moved more quickly; she felt a

slight drag on the phallus as if the walls of Jillian's vagina were expanding and contracting as the spasms inside became fiercer.

"I – I'm going to come!" Her voice went up high.

She squeezed as tightly as she could; felt the cock squirming, jerking in her hand almost as if it were real – then to complete the illusion, thick spurts of juice shot from the open slitted lips, hitting her face – then shooting again, thickly, sickeningly, obscenely. She watched, fascinated, as Jillian clutched and squeezed the reservoir at the phallus' base.

Jillian had dropped onto her back; her hand had slid off Alison's abused bottom. Now she raised and lowered her buttocks as the dregs of her lust flowed down her cock, squirted from the end onto Alison's face.

Crazily, Alison felt her clitoris jerking wildly when the thick droplets of juice hit her mouth. She slid out her tongue and tasted the thick, creamy fluid.

She looked at Jillian; her eyes were open and she was staring at her. "I... I'm sorry, Alison," she mumbled. "I really don't know what came over me then! Will you forgive me?"

Her words reminded her: Alison reached

to her bottom and felt the tender cheeks. They were flaming hot. "I – I'm all sore. My botty's so sore!"

"I – I'm sorry, Alison," she said again in a subdued tone of voice. Now that Alison had appeased her lust by masturbating her with the dildo, Jillian became quiet and apologetic. Perhaps I'm not the only one who's highly sexed around here, Alison said to herself.

"It'll hurt me to walk, I'm so sore!" Alison mumbled, exaggerating.

Jillian scrambled to her feet. "Please, Alison, put an arm around my shoulder. I'll help you back!"

They walked slowly back to Lazonby, the taller girl supporting the shorter.

"Why did you spank me like that?"

"I... I felt as if I owned you, as if you were my doll, my plaything," she mumbled. "I wanted to fuck your cunt and you wouldn't let me. So I spanked you because you were being 'naughty'!"

Alison shook her head impatiently. "But I mean – what makes you think that you have the right to do that?"

"Because Mummy told me... oh dear!"

"Told you what?"

"You're my present – she got you for me to play with!"

Alison gasped, still not quite comprehending. "What do you mean?"

"Mummy bought you for me for my birthday." She looked ashamed. "I'm nineteen years old. I hate boys of my age and the girls around here are really silly about sex. Mummy always said she'd buy me a sex companion – a real live doll, if you like – for my birthday!"

Alison's face was white with shock. So it would seem that I am a doll! Solely for the purpose of amusing, or being fucked by, this perverted young woman! It's crazy, crazy, crazy!

Alison walked the rest of the way in a kind of daze. Jillian supported her, tenderly, carefully – just as she was supposed to: after all, Alison was her very own little doll and she had to look after her. She knew. Her Mummy had told her!

Chapter 12

Hermione sat on the edge of her bed and looked at Alison with a cool, self-possessed expression on her face.

"What Jillian said is partly true, Alison, but – " she shrugged her shoulders, eloquently, "you've seen enough of Jillian to realise that she fantasises, imagines things, exaggerates…"

"She – she thinks I'm a doll," Alison blurted, "just for her own gratification – to do what she wants with – to use and abuse."

Hermione gave her a sharp look. "No one abuses you!"

"She spanked me," Alison retorted, "ripped off my panties and spanked me!"

"I saw her helping you toward the manor," said Hermione carefully, "holding you protectively as though you were something very precious, very important."

"That – that was after," Alison replied, her eyes flashing angrily.

Hermione glanced at a pile of bills that lay on her dresser. "I was counting the money," she said, softly. "Mr McEwen gave you forty pounds too much!" She fixed a penetrating gaze on Alison's face, "Why is that?"

Alison coloured. "That money's mine," she blurted. "I… I mixed my money with the rent money."

Hermione smiled, a slow, knowing smile. "Max gave it to you, didn't he, Alison?"

The colour drained out of Alison's face. "Well, yes, he did, but I…" she stammered.

"You don't have to explain," said

Hermione, coolly. "I know all about Max and the things he likes." She made her voice very soft. "Did you enjoy it? Forty pounds for doing something you liked can't be too bad!"

Alison didn't answer.

"But you don't have to be so bloody smug!" Hermione shot out. "Complaining about poor Jillian when you've just been jerking your randy pussy up and down on an old man's cock till he came." Then she added, softly, "For forty pounds, of course, I'm sure *that* made it all right!"

Alison jerked to her feet. "Stop it! What makes you think you can talk to me like this?"

Hermione looked mildly taken aback.

"Why, Alison – you're an employee of Lazonby Hall." Her voice was soft. "I can say what I like to you because I'm the mistress of the house. You work here – and *do what you're told*!" Her voice rose sharply on the last words.

"I don't have to stay here," Alison snapped. "I can walk right out... I don't have to put up with your half-witted daughter trying to rape me whenever she feels like it. I don't have to... "

"You don't have to do anything, do you, Alison?" Hermione put in coldly. "You can do whatever you like, can't you? But you liked it well enough when Jillian was waiting for you in your bedroom last night – you didn't come crying rape then!"

"You planned it that way," whispered Alison. "You – you got me worked up, watching what you were doing to Rosie and Sean, then you made me please you, satisfy you – then you left me up in the air – way up high and dry…"

"And dear Jillian was waiting for you in your room – with her big rubber toy all ready, no doubt – she was just what the doctor ordered, wasn't she, Alison?" Hermione spoke quickly.

"You planned it all!"

"But you enjoyed it!" Hermione's voice was sharp.

Alison was silent for a long moment, then said, "But I don't have to put up with being abused all the time. I – I…"

"Don't you get paid enough, Alison?" Hermione's voice was sugar-sweet. "Would you like more?"

"It's not the money," Alison muttered.

"Any extras you get – like from Max, you can keep, of course – that's all yours!"

"Well…"

"You have a choice," snapped Hermione, "staying or leaving; punishment or pleasure?"

Alison jerked her head up. "What d'you mean: punishment or pleasure?"

"I'll show you," said Hermione, giving Alison an enigmatic smile then touching the bell-push beside her bed.

Alison stared at the self-possessed woman in mingled confusion and shock; then there was a tap at the door.

"All right, come in," called Hermione.

Rosie and Sean entered, looking as though they'd been waiting for the summons.

They must have been outside the door all the time, Alison thought with fright. This is all premeditated! Is *everything* Hermione does so very well planned beforehand?

"Fasten her to the punishment stool," said Hermione, casually.

Alison's eyes jerked open wide. The stool!

"*No!*" she screamed. "I won't do it – no, no, *no!*"

Hermione lit a cigarette while Rosie dragged the strange stool from its place in the closet.

Alison made a lunge for the door, but Sean blocked her, regretfully but stolidly. "Relax, Miss Jeffreys," he murmured.

Miss Jeffreys! She felt like laughing hysterically.

They stripped off her skirt, removed her panties then tied her face down over the leather-covered stool. With vicious pleasure, Rosie tightened the straps that held her wrists and ankles in place.

"Get me the strap," said Hermione, and Alison's mind careened wildly. It isn't possible! This can't be happening to me! I've seen this happen to Rosie... but me, Alison, it isn't real!

"No, no, no!" she screamed. "Stop it – I want to go – I'm not staying here – Yiiiiiiih!" The high sound of fear spiralled from her lips.

"Please, Alison," said Hermione, patiently, "if you persist in screaming I'll have to gag your mouth – the sound is hurting my ears!"

"Relax, Miss Jeffreys," said Sean once more in his level voice.

She screamed again, and the sound seemed to excite Hermione. "See how her bottom squirms each time she screams," she hissed.

"Is this the right strap, Ma'am?" Sean asked.

"Yesss," Hermione hissed. "I don't want to break the skin – this two-inch thickness is perfect."

Petrified with fear, Alison heard the rustle of movement behind her; heard Rosie draw in her breath with an excited sound of anticipation... then the strap whistled through the air. The sharp pain cut through her buttocks, piercing from one sensitive cheek to the other then throbbing all over her bottom.

She screamed again, with rage as well as pain. How dare they do this to me!

The strap slashed down again, and she screamed again.

Again, the slap of the leather then the shrill sound from her lips.

Hazily, she remembered how Rosie had urinated when Hermione had punished her and, as the thought ran through her mind, she felt wetness between her thighs and knew that her bladder had reacted under the stress and pain in exactly the same way.

"Oh, please," she moaned, "no more – please!"

Miraculously, the slashing ceased.

"Such soft young flesh," Hermione whispered, then she felt fingers pinching her bottom, squeezing abused flesh cruelly but sensually and a stiff finger jabbed into her anus. "Saucy little arsehole," murmured Hermione. "She's a delicious piece of flesh. How could I ever let her go?"

There was a rustle of movement again, then Hermione snapped, "Is Doctor Maurice here yet?"

"Waiting outside, Ma'am," said Sean in his deferential voice.

"Have him come in," Hermione snapped.

Alison heard the sound of the door opening, then Hermione spoke to Rosie.

"Get the box from the dresser."

"Yes, Ma'am," said Rosie, eagerly, and Alison knew from the tone of the cook's voice that she was looking forward to jabbing an electrode into her sensitive anus, then sending in searing shocks.

"No," she moaned, "please, Hermione, not that!"

"Be patient, dear," said her mistress. "Punishment before pleasure!"

Rosie's voice was hungry. "Shall I stick it in her, Ma'am?"

"No!" Alison screamed. "Oh, no!"

"Proceed, Rosie," said Hermione, her voice calm. "Don't hurt her more than you have to!"

Alison felt as though her bottom was protruding up to the ceiling; she wanted to draw the cheeks in, contract her buttocks and make her small anus even smaller.

Rosie dabbed some sort of lubrication on the sensitive orifice, then probed at the slick opening with a finger; finally Alison felt the cool end of the electrode touching the inner flesh, then Rosie stabbed it in, deeply, cruelly.

Alison groaned, squirming with acute discomfort.

"Now turn on the current," said Hermione.

The jolt made her flatten her belly against the leather-covered stool; an agonising pain spiralled through her anus and into the base of her belly. To her deep shame, she lost control of her bladder again and hot urine splashed down between her thighs.

"Again," said Hermione, "just watch the pee squirt from her pussy – it's a most exciting sight!"

The fierce current throbbed through her flesh again, making her squeal with agony, bite at her lips and urinate again.

"Just one more," said Hermione.

This time Alison jerked herself up until only the straps kept her body from twisting off the stool. The shocks throbbed all over her, paralysing her throat so that she couldn't even scream any more.

"That'll be enough," said Hermione. "We don't want the poor girl to faint – we have so much more in store for her." Then she laughed, a sickening sadistic laugh.

"What are you doing?" It was Doctor Bell's voice.

"Ah, Maurice," said Hermione, "you've brought your appliance – your magic box?"

"Yes," he answered, "but what're you doing to this poor girl?"

"Make them stop!" Alison screamed. "They're torturing me, Doctor, make them stop!"

"It's just an experiment," said Hermione, coolly, "just like your tests!"

"My tests!" He sounded angry. "Release this young girl immediately – my tests provide pleasure, not pain!"

"That's why you're here, Maurice; you're going to provide the pleasure!" Hermione spoke soothingly.

"I'll have nothing to do with it," Maurice's voice was harsh. "I'm leaving – unfasten the girl and I'll drive her to the station!"

"*Maurice*!" Hermione's voice was like the crack of a whip. "You're forgetting something. I give the orders around here – not you! You do what you're told, Maurice, exactly what you're told, or else – " She stopped, ominously.

Alison heard the ex-doctor drawing in his breath, then when he spoke, his voice was strangely subdued. "What do you plan to do?"

'That's better," Hermione murmured. "Just excite her anus – gently, Maurice, bring her to a state of relaxed eroticism and then we'll untie her before we proceed any further."

"I don't like this," he muttered. "I don't like any part of it!"

"But you'll do it," said Hermione. "You know very well that you'll do it!"

Alison felt another hand touching her buttocks; gently this time, tenderly.

"Oh, Doctor," she moaned, "please don't hurt me – I've been hurt enough already!"

"Don't worry, my dear," he whispered, "this won't cause you any pain."

She felt him first withdraw one tube and then insert another up her sore back passage; almost as a reflex she tried to jerk away from the unbearable presence. It was in vain.

"Just keep still," he murmured. "You'll like this, Alison, really like it!" He pressed the electrode in more deeply, then she heard him step back.

In a moment, a soft, soothing current flowed into her anal opening and veered gently through her flesh, making it feel warm and causing her to forget the pain she'd suffered.

She drew in her thighs and squeezed them closed, trying to grip the tube with her pussy; it was thrilling her now, sending exciting stabs of pleasure zooming through her bottom.

"Ohhhh," she moaned, "ohhh!"

Hermione laughed. "She likes it; her sexed-up pussy's getting happy now!"

"Leave me alone for a minute," Maurice's voice was gruff. "I'll get her in the state you want in a few minutes but I want to do it without you here!"

There was a moment's silence, and Alison waited, feeling the soothing, sensual current pulsing into her body, thrilling her gently, relaxing her and making her fear diminish.

"Very well, Maurice," said Hermione. "Make sure you get her into the right state." She laughed shortly. "We'll leave you with your guinea pig. Come with me." And Alison heard movements as Rosie and Sean exited with Hermione.

She could hear him breathing before he spoke, "Feel better now?"

"Yes," Alison murmured, moving her bottom very slowly and feeling the electrode send out its magic throbs, "but – but why – why do you do anything she tells you?"

Maurice sighed. "There's nothing else I can do, Alison – she knows something about me; something that happened a long time ago, but she could use the knowledge to ruin my life if she wanted."

"Blackmail!" Alison hissed.

He gave a dry laugh. "More subtle than that! Very genteel pressure, veiled threats." His voice dropped down. "I can't afford to take a chance, Alison!"

She was silent, thinking about what he'd said: that explained some things that she hadn't understood. Hermione can force him to do anything she wants!

His hands went onto her buttocks and he lifted her higher on the bench.

"Relax your pussy," he murmured. She did as he told her, then the familiar electrode slid between her vaginal lips.

Alison drew in her breath when the first sweet shock rocked into her.

"Oooh," she murmured, "that's nice, Doctor."

"Don't call me Doctor," he muttered, "don't remind me – just call me Maurice."

But Alison was paying little attention to his words. The sensuous thrills were throbbing into her vulva, making her clitoris jerk and pulse with excitement. She wriggled her bottom and felt the thrilling current run from her anus to her pussy.

"It – it's going to make me come!" she hissed, her voice going high.

"Alison," Maurice said tensely, "would you like me to – to get inside you?"

He drew in a sobbing breath. "Would you

like me to fuck you while you're electrically aroused?"

"Oh, Maurice," Alison moaned, almost delirious with excitement, "you can do anything – anything you want!" She pressed back with her buttocks and he saw the tan orifice of her anus expanding round the tube.

His hands trembled when he ripped open his trousers, allowing his erect organ to burst out. He stood close behind her naked, writhing flesh then withdrew the tube from her pussy. Carefully, he steered his cock into the wet opening, feeling her vaginal walls close around his shaft, hugging it. His hand went to the knob that controlled the current flowing into her anus, and he turned it very gently. Alison gave a low moan of pleasure, and Maurice stood very still, feeling her pussy contracting as the mild shock ran through her flesh so that the soft walls hugged his cock more firmly. He increased the power; her pussy jerked closed, tightening its grip on his cock, then expanded, closed again.

Maurice closed his eyes and felt the sweat streaming down his face. This was the ultimate thrill: standing motionless feeling a juicy, young cunt suck, grip and hug his organ.

"I – I'm going to come," Alison gasped, squirming.

He could feel the head of his organ swelling, growing thicker and thicker until the walls gripped it like a snug velvet glove.

"Aaaah!" he groaned, starting to orgasm. "Alison – oh, Alison!"

Alison felt as though she might faint again: her pussy was vibrating, squeezing on the delicious cock that filled her hot, wet vulva.

"Ooohh!" she shrieked. "I can't stop myself. Ohhh, Maurice – I'm coming!"

The orgasm blasted through her body, making her pussy palpitate, sucking every last drop of the hot, spurting juice from Maurice's spitting cock. He turned the power up high, sending strong sensual waves jolting into her arsehole – then flowing through her body to her pussy until the current was transmitted to his cock.

The sex-juice drained out and he leaned forward limply. She was still writhing, squirming her buttocks and letting the soft, wet sounds drip from her lips.

"That was – was like heaven," she whispered. "Please do it again!"

The voice hit her ears like a thunderbolt. "I think you've had sufficient of Maurice's cock for now, Alison." Hermione gave her dry laugh.

"It's as I suspected, Maurice; you wanted

to sample her young pussy yourself." She added, "Again. Now," her voice became brisk, "complete the preparations on her body!"

"No," moaned Alison, "you're not going to hurt me again."

"Don't worry, Alison dear," said Hermione, "you've had your punishment – now it's time for your pleasure, as I promised."

Dazed, still experiencing a sweet sensation from the residue of the electrical treatment, Alison felt Rosie and Sean unfastening the straps which bound her, then leading her to the bed.

She was completely nude now, her blouse having been removed at the start of the punishment session, and her breasts felt heavy, the nipples stiff and demanding.

They had sat her on the edge of the bed; now, she dropped onto her back, passing her hand across her nipples.

Hermione stared at the naked, sensuous flesh, then she licked at her lips with quick flicks of her tongue.

"Her body's still hungry," she whispered. She moved up close, reached down and touched the top of Alison's slit.

She flinched when Hermione's finger touched her clitoris.

"Oohhh," she moaned, "oohhhh – I'm on fire all over!" She touched her breasts again, then squeezed at the nipples.

"Rosie!" Hermione snapped. "Eat her nipples!" She leaned over Alison. "There's no one, absolutely no one, my dear, who can lick nipples as exquisitely as Rosie!"

The cook moved onto the bed and lay at Alison's side.

Alison looked into her face with momentary fear. "You – you hate me, don't you?" she mumbled.

Rosie smiled. "No, Miss – " Her lower lip quivered. "Maybe I'm envious because you're so young and enticing." She moved her face over Alison's breasts, then added, "Because everyone wants to do things to you – to your luscious, young body – " her eyes went onto Alison's as she added in a whisper, "even me!" Then her mouth went down and she drew a nipple between her lips, sweetly and sensuously, and tickled the tip with her tongue. Alison sighed, then felt someone doing something between her open thighs.

"It's all right," said Maurice's voice when Alison jerked. "I'm inserting the electrode." She felt the tube sliding into her vulva and opened her thighs wider, sighing with pleasurable anticipation.

Rosie's mouth was doing delicious things

to her nipples now, switching from one to the other, keeping them both at a throbbing peak of excitement. When she wasn't kissing one, she squeezed it with her clever fingers, then reversed and repeated the process.

The electrode was gradually increasing the strength of its thrilling waves inside her pussy and Alison was experiencing a euphoric, all-embracing sensation of sensuality in all parts of her body. *This is worth waiting for – this is pure heaven!* The thought flickered in her mind and she squirmed, feeling every part of her body alive and aware.

"You're enjoying this, aren't you?" Hermione murmured as she seated herself on the bed and looked into Alison's face.

Alison jerked open her eyes and a momentary haze of fear shielded them.

"Why – why are you doing this to me?"

"Don't you like it?"

"Oh, yes," Alison sighed, "but why?" She moved her breasts and felt Rosie's soft lips caressing the nipples with delicious persistence.

"Because I want to show you how nice things can be. I want you to see that you can have a lot of pleasure here... because I want you to stay with us."

Alison blinked, thinking about the

strange, sensuous but exciting woman's words.

"Do you want to stay at Lazonby?" Hermione asked.

A deep throb jolted from the electrode to the top of her vulva and Alison felt her clitoris vibrate. "Oooohh," she moaned, "oooooh – *oooohh*!"

"What are you thinking about now?" Hermione asked.

Alison screwed shut her eyes and considered the question. "My – my pussy," she whispered at last. "How it's throbbing... it keeps coming to the – the brink of an orgasm, then dying down, then rising up again. It's wonderful – and my breasts are on fire, all throbbing at the tips!"

"What else would you like? What else is in your mind? What do you see when you screw shut your eyes?" Hermione hissed into Alison's face.

The colour heated Alison's cheeks. A cock! I want a cock in my pussy! She squirmed. A thick, massive cock!

"I – I want," she stammered, "a – a *cock*!" She opened her eyes and watched Hermione's expression.

"Can you see it in your mind? Can you see what you want?" Hermione's voice was tense and tight.

Alison closed her eyes again and drew her eyebrows together in a frown of concentration. I can see it! A huge, monstrous thing – black and gleaming – and it keeps swelling, getting bigger, while the balls beneath are heavy with cream! The thrills seemed to flow through her flesh with renewed intensity. I want it now! I need it – I want to be fucked – right now!

Alison kept her eyes closed, seeing the massive balls behind the thick cock – then above them, high up, the face of the man – no boy – no... girl! The handsome, fresh-faced visage of... Jillian! She jerked open her eyes.

"Is this it?" Hermione asked, pointing one end of the huge, black, rubber double dildo at Alison's face.

"Is it Jillian's cock that you want?" And the attractive, young lesbian smiled down at Alison, desire and humour in her eyes while her mother held her cock so delicately and pointed it at the face of the girl she was going to let her daughter fuck.

"Yes!" Alison whispered. "That's it!" And she opened her legs wider and felt Hermione pulling out the electrode, then Jillian dropped onto her belly and the massive shaft drove into her, thrilling her and bringing her to an intense, throbbing orgasm while Rosie still sucked her nipples.

* * *

"You see," said Hermione afterward, "there are so many things here that you like." She smiled at Alison. Jillian had left the room with Maurice and Sean while Rosie was busy, smearing a new, exotic kind of cream on every sensual part of Alison's still-naked body.

"Yes," Alison murmured, "I can see that." Her eyes clouded, momentarily.

"But I was frightened, Hermione, when you did those terrible things to me!"

"But they thrilled you in the end!"

"But they hurt me, really scared me!"

"Punishment before pleasure," Hermione murmured, "but the pleasure's worth all that goes before." She paused, then said, "But that won't ever be necessary again, will it?"

"I don't think so," whispered Alison.

"So you'll stay here!" There was relief in Hermione's voice.

Alison drew her brows together. "I don't think there's anything else I can do," she squirmed, "the way I feel – all sensuous and aroused... I get worked up so quickly that I have to have relief!"

"It's always available here," murmured Hermione.

"Yes," said Alison, "I can see that!"

"I've wanted to have someone like you with me for a long time," said Hermione, "but I doubted that I'd ever find the person I wanted."

Alison stared at her mistress.

"You're very much like me, you know," Hermione smiled down at her.

Alison's mouth dropped open in surprise.

"And you'll be much more so when you're older!"

"Why do you say that?" gasped Alison.

Hermione smiled. "I can tell." She took a deep breath. "I'm not as young as I was – and I worry about Jillian sometimes. If I wasn't here, God knows what might happen to her – they might even put her away in some institution. The poor girl might really go out of her mind then. Of course if you were here – " she looked at Alison very intently, "– as a legal guardian, in charge of the manor, there wouldn't be any problem."

"Don't talk like that, Hermione. You're all right – what makes you think that something would happen to you?"

Hermione smiled. "Nothing really, I'm just thinking out loud – and I want to know how you feel about the idea."

Alison moved herself gently as Rosie

massaged a very sensitive part of her body. "I – I don't know what to say, Hermione. I don't even like to think about it!" Her eyes were troubled.

"That's all right," Hermione reassured her. "I intend to be around for a long time yet – but I want to be sure you'll stay!"

"I'll stay, Hermione, I promise. I want to stay – there doesn't seem to be anything else I want to do!"

Hermione hesitated, then said, "And Jillian – what about her?"

Alison stared at Hermione. "You – you mean her being after me all the time, trying to get into my pussy?"

"That's what I mean," Hermione said.

"I don't mind," said Alison. She giggled. "In fact, I'm beginning to quite like it!"

Hermione smiled. "I thought you would," she whispered. "You're a dear girl, Alison, a very sweet girl!"

Alison smiled back, then a dreamy expression came onto her face. "Jillian does have an – an amazing variety of cocks!" She giggled.

Hermione nodded. "Yes. I know just how amazing!"

Alison looked at her face slyly. "I'm sure you do!"

Hermione laughed. "And unlike some

men's I've known, they're always in a state of erection; always ready!"

"So I've noticed."

"Just a glimpse under your skirt – just one little hair of your pussy makes her want to masturbate."

"I guessed that!"

"She even masturbates at the dinner table!"

"I've seen her," Alison admitted.

Hermione looked at Alison, fondly. "I think you'll fit in perfectly here."

Alison nodded. "I'm beginning to think that, too."

"The money," said Hermione, "you can save just about all I pay you – and then there are extras – "

"Like Max McEwen?"

Hermione laughed. "Like that – and I'm sure there'll be more if you want it!"

Alison was thoughtful, then said, "And Doctor Maurice?"

"He'll always be here," said Hermione, "whenever you want to see him, he'll be ready." She met Alison's eyes, "He'll do anything you want – anything!"

"That'll be nice," murmured Alison. "I like him."

"He's downstairs now," said Hermione. "I'll go down and invite him to stay for dinner."

Rosie's hands did delicious things between Alison's thighs.

"And Alison," said Hermione, "tonight –" she hesitated.

"Yes?"

Hermione took a deep breath. "Would you like to have Maurice stimulate both of us, and after – " she wet her lips, "we'll spend the night together in my bed?"

A new kind of excitement throbbed through Alison's body. She had never really experienced the delights of an older, more experienced, woman's body.

"There are some – some new things I could show you, perhaps," murmured Hermione, her voice strangely unsteady.

"Oh, yes," hissed Alison, "oh, Hermione, yes!"

Alison followed Hermione with her eyes as the older woman left the bedroom.

Rosie's strong cook's hands massaged and kneaded Alison's sensitive flesh, silently, thoroughly.

"Deeper!" muttered Alison, squirming her young flesh. "Dig in deep, keep me aroused, touch every throbbing part of me – make me come and come and come because I can never have enough. The more I get, the more I want. Appease me, Rosie, now!"

And Alison twisted herself onto her face

as the cook's skilful, experienced hands did voluptuous things to every sensuous part of her erotic body.

ENVOI – SIX MONTHS LATER...

The drawing-room at Lazonby had been transformed. The heavy curtains were drawn, furniture had been moved, armchairs and sofas pushed back to the walls, tables and chairs likewise. With only a few table lamps lit, and a wood fire blazing in the grate, the big, formal room looked uncharacteristically warm and inviting on this cold winter's evening.

On the whole, the supper party had been a success, thought Alison. However, now she and the others were looking forward to the evening's main entertainment: the disciplining of a member of the staff. For once, Sean and Rosie were not the subjects of this discipline: it was a new member of staff, Marie, a pretty redheaded girl from France who had been taken on as housemaid only weeks before. The vivacious eighteen-year-old had already been subjected to Dr Bell's exhaustive tests and had responded exceptionally well. But only the other day she had broken one of a pair of Hermione's favourite china figurines, smashed beyond repair and quite irreplaceable. In Hermione's opinion, the standards of the staff were becoming far too lax: Marie's punishment tonight promised to be exemplary.

When the two male guests entered, Maurice Bell pushing Max McEwen in his wheelchair, Alison and the other two women of the house, Hermione and Jillian, were already lounging on huge cushions by the fireplace, having left the dining-room first, as tradition dictated. The women had changed for the evening's next entertainment. Alison was wearing her sheer, nylon, baby doll nightie. Hermione was dressed in her thigh-length leather boots, short leather skirt and, tonight, a matching leather halter that left little to the imagination: two holes exposed her large, prominent nipples, 'peek-a-boo' style. Jillian was also dressed provocatively: she wore a mini-kilt, and nothing else, giving her the appearance of a young Amazon.

The men must feel positively overdressed, smiled Alison to herself as she let her fingers play through Jillian's thick crop, tickling her earlobes and even letting a finger stray across her lips, which half-opened so that she could enter the warm, wet cavern of her mouth. Hermione was busy with fingers and tongue between Alison's wide-spread thighs, causing her young secretary to moan occasionally with pleasure, while Jillian was idly masturbating her own pussy, already saturated in anticipation of the events to come.

Maurice and Max looked on with obvious pleasure, and eventually both of them got their clothes off, Alison getting up to assist the paralytic with his trousers and underwear. By now the group was naked and ready for the punishment to commence. Hermione pressed the little bell-push by the fireplace and almost immediately the three servants entered the room: a pale and anxious-looking Marie, still in her staff uniform of black dress and white, lace-trimmed pinafore, was flanked by Rosie and Sean, both naked. Alison noted that Sean's big cock, that bobbed and weaved in front of him, was massively erect. But then, she thought, suppressing a bubbly giggle, so are the other two men's!

Marie was led in silence to a curious chair in the middle of the room. Ironically, its original purpose had been for prayer: it had been designed with a low, padded seat for kneeling and a padded top for praying in comfort, but now, by simply reversing this piece of furniture, it became a padded whipping chair. The victim was bent over and her wrists were tied to the front legs of the chair by Sean, while Rosie lifted the now blushing young maid's skirt to reveal a beautifully plump posterior. Alison watched as the girl's two fleshy buttocks contracted and relaxed spasmodically as she anxiously awaited her punishment. Aware that her anus and downy vulva were on display for all to see, the young redhead was blushing prettily.

Hermione stood up, her shapely figure outlined against the glow of the fire.

"Jillian, dear, it's time you took some of your duties and responsibilities seriously as heiress to Lazonby. Among these is the disciplining of staff. You will administer Marie's punishment with twenty lashes of the strap."

So saying she handed Jillian the thick leather strap and the lithe young girl positioned herself behind the whimpering, dreadfully exposed maid. Without further ado, she started to lay into the bound girl's bottom with a vengeance. It came as no surprise to Alison that the aggressive young lesbian took her punishment duties so seriously: by the fifth stroke, Marie was already begging her young mistress to stop.

"Please, I entreat you, *Mademoiselle*, I will do anything you ask... I beg you, please stop...!"

But Jillian was enjoying herself too much to stop and gradually the stripes on Marie's bottom criss-crossed and multiplied until her voluptuous, rounded buttocks glowed – first a light blush, then a deep pink, and finally, by the time the last lash of the strap was administered, an angry, suffused red.

Marie was sobbing and had all but collapsed over the chair's back. Maurice Bell, as always, was concerned, and got up to see if he could do anything to alleviate the poor girl's suffering, but Jillian was merciless and waved him back.

"Sean," she beckoned, "come over here and get ready to fuck this girl silly! She's had the pain and now she can get some pleasure – and you look as though you could provide it," she added with a smirk, glancing at his engorged, twitching erection.

But as Sean stood behind Marie, positioning his achingly stiff penis at the split of the sobbing young girl's sex, and preparing to do his young mistress' bidding, Jillian herself was in for the shock of her life. At a signal from Hermione, Rosie and Alison each took her by the arm and, before she could protest, marched her over to where Max sat in his wheelchair, his long, thin cock standing perpendicular. With a motion so fluid it might well have been rehearsed, they lifted the struggling girl on top of the paralysed, but virile, old man. Alison deftly took hold of Max's cock and placed it at the entrance to Jillian's already wet vagina while Hermione held her daughter's hips and manoeuvred her downwards onto the vertical shaft.

"No-o-o-o!" screamed Jillian in a long, drawn-out wail, "I don't want his horrible man's thing inside me!"

"Disciplining the staff, dear," soothed her mother, "is not the most important of your responsibilities. You must learn to appreciate the male sex, as well as the female. Now it's your duty to ensure the continuance of the long line of Simpsons at Lazonby." And with this, she pushed down hard on her daughter's shoulders so that the girl was suddenly impaled to the hilt on Max's impressive erection.

"Oh, Mummy!" cried Jillian with a hurt look of betrayal on her features. "How could you... How could you possibly do this to me?"

Involuntarily, her arms went around Max's neck in order to keep her balance.

"I haven't finished yet, my girl!" answered Hermione with a grim smile.

"Maurice! Do what you have to!"

Alison watched as the handsome, middle-aged doctor moved in behind Jillian, holding a rigid penis that appeared far too large for its destination, which she assumed could only be Jillian's tight little arsehole. Of course! Hermione wants her to experience two cocks at the same time! It's kill or cure for the young lesbian, she thought. She glanced over at Marie and Sean. The stocky chauffeur was now plunging his cock hard into the poor girl, but she seemed to be enjoying it well enough, lustily thrusting her inflamed bottom back at him with every shove he gave, as if the lashing she had received had heightened the pleasure of being ravished by the chauffeur. His hands had somehow managed to free her full breasts and he was squeezing them as he drove his prick into the flame-haired maid's wet, tight vagina, pinching her swollen red nipples hard so that she gasped with delight.

"Oh, *Monsieur Sean*, that feels... wonderful!" she said in a low, husky voice. "Please don't ever stop!"

Watching, Alison stole a hand between her thighs and started to play with herself gently, inflamed by the sight of both Jillian and Marie, aroused as much by the former's outraged squawks of protest as by the latter's deep sighs of pleasure. She saw herself momentarily in bed, naked, with the two girls, writhing in an ecstasy of sexual pleasure between them...

"Alison!" said Hermione Simpson sharply.

The young secretary was dragged back to reality by her employer.

"Prepare Jillian's arsehole for fucking!"

Alison was shocked at the request, for she knew that Hermione meant her to lick Jillian's anus until it was lubricated enough to accept Dr Bell's large penis. But Hermione's delivery of this bizarre request in such crude language was no surprise to Alison: in a situation such as this, the mistress of Lazonby would often use language better suited to a brothel than to a drawing-room, and her aristocratic tones made it only more piquant.

"That's right, get down there and lick her little, brown hole!"

With a small grimace, Alison stuck out her small, pink tongue until it connected with the puckered orifice. She licked it tentatively, only relieved that Jillian was so punctilious about her personal hygiene. Despite herself, Jillian groaned with pleasure. She saw, at very close quarters, the shaft of Max's penis disappearing and reappearing into the cleft of Jillian's vulva below. She noticed that the young lesbian was still lubricating freely and, indeed, seemed to be causing all the movement herself, rising and falling upon the old man as if she were secretly enjoying this new experience. Alison warmed to her task, sticking her tongue into Jillian's anal hole as far as the tight sphincter would allow her to; she could taste the tangy female juices that were spreading in the widely-stretched valley of Jillian's buttocks, and occasionally flicked her tongue downwards to where Max's long, thin cock was spearing into the almost virgin territory of Jillian's cunt.

Alison glanced behind her. In order to ensure that Maurice Bell's erection was sustained, Hermione had knelt down and was busy sucking and licking the spongy head of his sizeable phallus. She took it into her mouth and swirled her tongue around the turgid head. Above, Rosie was feeding her voluptuous breasts to the eager, greedy lips of Max McEwen. The cook's large, sensitive nipples were lightly bitten and nibbled so as to send her into a frenzy of excitement. Everyone's occupied now, she thought happily. No one's been left out.

Hermione gently pushed her out of the way and replaced her presence behind Jillian with Maurice Bell's cock, which she carefully introduced to her daughter's tight, little bottom hole. As she watched the doctor's penis slowly disappear between the groaning, bucking lesbian's bottom cheeks, Alison suffered a little pang of jealousy. I want my pussy and arsehole to be filled too! I'm feeling so randy... anyone... anything would do... but... everyone was busy, she thought sadly as she moved away from the writhing, moaning little group.

Her employer must have caught the wistful look on Alison's face, for suddenly Hermione was lying down on the carpet in front of the fire, tightening the straps of her daughter's monstrous black phallus and once more beckoning her.

She held the well-oiled dildo so that it pointed straight up. Alison was mesmerised by the sight and ran a needy, but anxious, tongue over dry lips.

"Now strip, Alison; take that frilly thing off, come over here, kneel over me and sit on it, girl," she commanded. "But you must put it up your bottom!"

Alison looked stunned. The enormity of the idea! Could she really mean...

As if reading her thoughts, Hermione spat out: "Yes, I mean your arsehole, girl, and hurry up about it!"

Now entirely naked, Alison gritted her teeth and sank down onto the huge artificial penis, trying to relax her tight sphincter as she nudged its head into her anal hole.

"Oh-h-h," she groaned as she impaled herself slowly on the monster. She could feel Hermione's hands on her hips, pulling her down, gently but firmly.

"That's right, my dear," husked Hermione in an altogether more gentle tone, "now, start fucking, that's it, up and down, up and down…"

For a while Alison rose and fell, buggering herself upon the large, solid shaft of the dildo, feeling little fulfilment from this strange, painful invasion of her rectum. She felt exposed and more than a little self-conscious as she faced the other two groups, impaled as she was on Hermione's huge, artificial penis, acutely aware that her pussy was obscenely, gapingly displayed to the others.

Sean watched as the young secretary bucked up and down on the sodomising black phallus, her thighs wide open and her delectable pink vulva temptingly displayed among the dark curls of her pubic bush. He gave one final, brutal thrust into Marie's dripping cunt then pulled his cock out of her completely. The French maid moaned in frustration as he disengaged himself from her, even clutching wildly behind her as if to pull him back in. But the Irishman had different

ideas: he came over to where Alison was awkwardly jigging herself up and down, his stiff, nearly perpendicular cock, still shiny with the redhead's copious juices, bobbing and swaying in front of him.

"Now, Miss Jeffreys, I think you need a little more attention: that lovely cunt of yours looks in need of filling... don't you think so, Madam?" This last was addressed respectfully to his employer as she lay beneath Alison, bucking her hips upwards continually so that the dildo flashed in and out of her secretary's rectal cave in a fluid motion.

"Yes, Sean, fuck the little bitch, she needs it, badly – can't you see – her pussy's streaming wet! I can feel her juices on my fingers."

Alison blushed a little: it was true, the constant arse-fucking that she was experiencing had begun to take effect. No longer causing her any pain or discomfort, the sensations in her bottom were now deeply pleasurable and her pussy was beginning to throb and tingle, aching to be filled.

Hermione Simpson groped between Alison's wide-spread thighs and, when she had located the girl's hairy outer lips, took hold of them between her delicate fingers and pulled them open, so that Sean had an even easier target for his achingly stiff manhood. Alison resigned herself to her fate a little fearfully, leaning back so that her head was next to Hermione's; she was able to feel the older woman's hot breath on her cheek and her full, firm breasts as they bored into her naked back. Sean knelt between her widely-splayed thighs; first he stroked her convulsing belly and squeezed her tender breasts, rolling the stiff nipples between his rough fingers. Then with one determined thrust, he brutally shoved his sex far up Alison's hotly clasping vaginal tunnel.

"*Ah-h-h-rgh!*" she cried out as the chauffeur's big penis entered her and filled her completely, its head bumping her cervix. But it was a cry of pure, unadulterated pleasure. Alison had never even dreamed that this double penetration could be so wonderful: for several minutes the two shafts thrust in and out of her with just a thin dividing wall between them; as she writhed and bucked, her body racked by the early spasms of a massive, approaching climax, Hermione barked out a final command, "Marie, get over here and squat down over Miss Jeffreys' face!"

The French maid looked momentarily puzzled; her grasp of English was not perfect.

"*Madame*?"

"Get your cunt over her mouth, you silly young bitch!"

Marie scampered over to where Alison was buffeted between the chauffeur and her employer and, bending her legs, slowly squatted down so that her streaming pussy, its surrounding pubic bush copper-coloured, dark and matted with her juices, descended upon Alison's up-thrust face.

As Alison's tongue flicked out to lick at the redhead's dripping, swollen pussy flesh, her orgasm exploded throughout her body; the young secretary screamed in ecstatic release. Above her, Marie gasped as she felt her clitoris come into contact with eager lips and tongue – this alone was enough to send the young maid into paroxysms of delight. An orgasmic frenzy gripped them all: Sean groaned as his heavy balls tightened and his cock spewed rope after rope of thick, white semen deep into the clasping channel of Alison's vagina, while below Hermione let out a high-pitched, keening wail of pleasure as she climaxed repeatedly.

The four of them lay there shuddering with intense delight as the final tremors of their mutual orgasms subsided. Eventually Sean pulled his dribbling cock out of Alison with a lewd sucking noise and, as she struggled upwards, Hermione's rubbery dildo also slipped noisily out of her brutally stretched anus. A rivulet of semen trickled down her inner thigh as she stepped shakily to her feet and looked around.

She glanced over to the other foursome as they inexorably approached their own crisis, the near-hermaphroditic figure of Jillian straining towards total fulfilment as she bucked and squirmed on the impaling cocks of the two rutting males while Rosie fed her the tips of her big-nippled breasts. Alison smiled wearily but contentedly. Life at Lazonby was all right. No, it was better than just 'all right'. It was very, very good. In fact, it was damn near perfect.

THE END